THE WALLFLOWER'S CHOICE

WALTZING WITH WALLFLOWERS (BOOK 6)

ROSE PEARSON

THE WALLFLOWER'S
CHOICE

PROLOGUE

"Quite frankly, I do not think that your sister should even have permitted you to attend this wedding." Prudence swallowed hard, her stomach twisting sharply. She had no answer for that, for her mother's words were quite correct. She had done a great deal to injure her sister and her now husband, and it had all come from a place of utter selfishness. "The fact that you stood there beside her, watching her marry Lord Newling, speaks of their forgiving hearts and their generous spirits," Lady Lymington continued, her lip curling just a little as she turned towards Prudence again. "I hope that you will never do such a foolish thing again."

Tears sprang into Prudence's eyes and though she nodded, she could not hold her mother's gaze, looking away instead. Part of her hoped that her mother would speak softly to her, that there would come a tenderness, and perhaps even an understanding, now that she had berated her but, instead, Lady Lymington let out a small exclamation and, turning on her heel, went out of the drawing room and left Prudence alone.

The pain which lanced through Prudence's heart was so great that it was difficult for her to contain herself. Tears began to drop to her cheeks and Prudence covered her face with her hands, sinking down into the soft cushions of the couch behind her.

I have never felt more alone.

The difficulty was, Prudence recognized, that this was all her own doing. She had been the one who had tried to force Lord Newling into marrying *her* rather than marrying her sister. She had seen that Frederica, her sister, had been falling in love with the gentleman, and had found herself torn apart by a burning, furious jealousy which had driven her to work all the harder to force his hand. She had set up a situation not once, but twice in the hope of ensnaring him and yet, she had been found out and had not had any other choice but to admit to it all.

At the time, Prudence had believed herself to be entirely justified in doing as she had done, for she was the eldest daughter, and it was quite right for the eldest to make the best match that she could, before the younger sought a match of her own. She had been frustrated by her father's lack of interest in putting *her* first, rather than attempting to secure them both a suitable husband and had, at the end of it all, come to a sense of deep anger that she had not been able to succeed.

Now, however, she did not feel even the smallest hint of anger or frustration. Instead, she felt nothing but shame and mortification, wanting to hide herself away from society, and even from her own family. Her mother had berated her almost constantly for what she had done, reminding her of her failings, repeating to her all of the foolish things that she had done and said, so that the weight of it continued to hang over her head. It did not matter that Prudence was truly repentant, that her sorrow was genuine, and her distress ever present, Lady Lymington was quite determined to make her aware of just how much shame she had brought upon the family.

Dropping her hands to her lap, Prudence pulled out her handkerchief and dabbed at her eyes. The tears continued to fall, however, and her chest was tight with sobs as she looked back on all that she had done, and felt herself broken over it. How grateful she was to Frederica and Lord Newling for their forgiveness! She knew it was undeserved, given all that she had done, but they had been willing to offer it to her anyway. There was still hurt, still a brokenness in their relationship which her actions had brought about, but both Frederica and Lord Newling had wanted to make it quite clear that they held no grudge against her. That was why they had insisted that she be a part of the wedding day.

It was difficult for me to hold my head up there, Prudence thought to herself as her tears finally began to dry on her cheeks. *Even the good Lord above knows what I have done.*

The door opened and Prudence, unable to bear another word of disappointment from her mother, dropped her head, praying that Lady Lymington would not see her tears.

"There you are, Prudence."

Prudence looked up in surprise, seeing her father coming in to join her.

"Papa."

"You did very well today." A kind smile on his face, Lord Lymington sat down on the couch beside her and reached out to press her hand. "I think that you found it all a little trying, did you not?" Unable to help the tears which flooded her eyes again, Prudence nodded but said nothing, her throat contracting. "I am sorry for that, though you must often bring to mind that Lord and Lady Newling hold nothing against you. There has been a healing between all of you, especially since you admitted your wrongdoing and it became clear that you feel regret over what you did."

"I am so sorry," Prudence whispered, unable to trust her voice. "I did not think–"

"You do not need to keep apologizing," her father interrupted, squeezing her hands as his expression gentled. "Please, my dear, do not think that I expect anything more from you. You have said enough! You have made amends to the best of your ability, and I can see that your heart is truly contrite."

Prudence closed her eyes and fresh tears fell.

"Mama does not see it so."

"Your mother is very upset," Lord Lymington answered, though his voice had dropped a little. "I will speak to her, for I can see that this continued reminder of your failings has pained you." He pressed her hand again and then cleared his throat. "Now, what say you to the idea that we return to London next Season and find *you* a match?"

Prudence blinked furiously, and her breath caught in her chest, as she tried to let her father's words sink in.

"You look surprised." Lord Lymington smiled gently. "You did not think that we would leave you to be a spinster, did you?"

"But I do not deserve such consideration," Prudence replied, her voice still a little hoarse. "Papa, I did so many things that were wrong, I cannot think why you would show me such a kindness."

Lord Lymington let out a small sigh, shook his head and then looked at Prudence for a long moment without speaking. When he did speak again, there was a gentle tenderness in both his voice and his expression which healed a few of the wounds of Prudence's sorrowful heart.

"My dear Prudence, you have done wrong, yes, but your sister and her husband have forgiven it. Your mother and I do not want you to be unhappy. We want you to have the same happiness as Frederica, and we would not withhold that from you."

"But I am still a wallflower," Prudence told him, closing her eyes as a fresh wave of tears threatened. "The first time I was found in close quarters with Lord Newling, the *ton* believed that I was at fault, and so have rejected me. And now I am sure that society knows of my wicked actions and will turn from me all the more."

Her father shook his head.

"The *ton* does not know of it all, Prudence," he said, making Prudence's heart leap with a sudden hope. "You may believe it to be so, but I can assure you that you are wrong. The *ton* has no knowledge about your attempts to force a betrothal between yourself and Lord Newling. The only thing they know is that a wallflower has now married Lord Newling and, I must say, I hope that fact will stand you in good stead now."

"What do you mean?"

Her father shrugged.

"Your sister is now Lady Newling. We are a well-connected family and with this additional connection, I must pray that the *ton* will, once more, choose to accept you as you are."

Prudence dropped her head, an ache building in her chest. She could not quite take in her father's generosity towards her, could not quite accept that there was to be such forgiveness from him – and an encouragement to her to thereafter go in search of her own happiness. She felt as though she did not deserve any of it, so weighed down was she by the heaviness of her guilt.

"I am certain that, when the Season comes again, you will be able to return to London with a greater confidence than you have had before," Lord Lymington said quietly, releasing Prudence's hand and getting to his feet. "We will wait for the autumn and the winter to come and to pass and, thereafter, we will return to London together and do our level best to find you an excellent gentleman to marry." Bending down just a little, he put one hand on Prudence's shoulder. "Do not let your prior mistakes burn through you day after day after day. Look to the future, my dear Prudence. It is going to be a good deal brighter than the struggle you have now, I assure you." With a smile, Lord Lymington made his way to the door, opened it, and stood in the doorway. "I will have a tea tray sent to you, my dear. I think that you could do with a little refreshment."

Prudence managed to smile as her father nodded and then stepped away, leaving her to consider all that he had said. She got to her feet and went across the room to stand at the window, looking out at her father's grand estate. For so long, she had felt nothing but heaviness within herself, a sadness which had never once faded. Now, however, there was a tiny flicker of hope which began to burn within her. Hope that she *might* be given another chance to find a suitable match for herself, hope that there could be a little happiness in her future.

Though I am still a wallflower, as I said to Papa.

That thought made Prudence drop her head, her shoulders rounding as fresh tears began to burn at the edges of her eyes. It was her fault that she was a wall-flower, her fault that she was no longer encouraged to step into society. Could there truly be any sort of relief for her? Any chance of being seen as a true member of the *ton* rather than being asked to stand back and hide in the shadows?

"I do not deserve it," she mumbled to herself, managing to blink back her tears. Her guilt was still much too great, her heart still weighed with regret and sorrow. Could she have even the smallest hope that she might find happiness? Or would the weight of regret and shame push her down, hold her back, and keep her away as a consequence of all the wicked things she had done?

CHAPTER ONE

*P*rudence licked her lips and clasped her hands together as she looked out at the ballroom. This was her first time back in London and, though the invitations had begun to arrive, that had not filled Prudence with any sense of confidence that all would be well. She did not know whether or not the *ton* would welcome her back, whether what she had done last Season would still be remembered and, if it was, what society would expect from her.

The only way she would know for certain would be to step forward and attempt to insert herself back into society again, trying to converse with other gentlemen and ladies in the hope that they would speak with her.

I cannot do it.

Taking a deep breath, Prudence set her shoulders and lifted her chin. She tried to take a step forward, attempting to follow her mother and father, who had given her the time and the space she required before making her way further into the ballroom, but she could not do it. It was as though invisible strings were holding her back, tugging her back into the shadows she knew so well. Lowering her head, Prudence fought against the sense of despair that immediately began to crash over her.

Yes, she had endured being a wallflower before but, at that time, she had been utterly determined to catch Lord Newling, so it had not mattered to her. She had not cared about being back amongst the other wallflowers and had deliberately set herself apart from them, choosing to be alone rather than with the others who might understand her predicament and could share in her sorrows. Given that her only intention had been to tie herself to Lord Newling by whatever means she could, Prudence had not given a single thought to the fact that she was no longer welcomed by society, that they ignored her and forgot entirely about her presence.

She had told herself repeatedly that it would not matter in her future, for she would soon be wed, and all of the *ton* would be glad to welcome her then! That had been her plan, her intention, and her expectation, and all of it had fallen apart. She now had nothing save for her own company. There was no husband to speak of, no respect from the *ton,* no awareness of her presence as she set foot in amongst them again. Barely anyone had even glanced at her and, as Prudence twisted her fingers together, she felt herself shrink inwardly. Her father had promised that the *ton* did not know of what she had tried to do. They were entirely unaware that she had done her best to force Lord Newling into a situation where they could be discovered, with matrimony being the only way forward for both of them. Could she be sure of that?

What if someone from society had overheard one of her conversations with either Lord Newling or her sister? What then? Even if she dared make herself step forward, then what might she be met with?

"I am sure I was not this weak before."

Prudence shook her head to herself, irritated and upset with how little courage she had. She wanted to hurry away, to stand tall and place a smile on her lips but she could not bring herself to do either thing. Instead, the shadows made her welcome, wrapping around her shoulders as a friend might do. Prudence took another step back and let out a long, slow breath of regret.

The consequences of what she had done had not fallen on either Lord Newling or on Frederica and, given how she now felt about her actions, Prudence was glad of that. All the same, however, she felt herself filled with a fresh wave of sorrow and regret. Had she chosen to behave properly, had she chosen to simply let her sister pursue Lord Newling and looked for another gentleman herself, none of this would have happened. And perhaps then, she might have found herself happiness already, might have been contented at home, setting up in her new life as mistress of her husband's home.

Instead, all she was left with was darkness.

"Oh, excuse me! I did not see you there."

Prudence stepped back, only for the gentleman to laugh and sway forward, his glass of wine teetering a little too close to her. He had only just barreled into her, clearly in his cups, and much too drunk to have any real understanding about what he was doing. His speech was a little slurred, his smile slipping as he saw her frown and, much to Prudence's astonishment, he reached out one hand towards her.

"You do not need to look like that, now," he said, his eyebrows furrowing. "You do not look pleased to see me and everyone in the *ton* is usually pleased to see me."

"Is that so?"

Prudence spoke mildly, doing her best to feign an interest while silently wondering where her mother and father had gone. If they were close by, then she would hurry to them at once or, if she could catch her mother's eye, would silently beg of her to draw near. This gentleman was a little too bold and brash to Prudence's mind, to the point that a warning began to ring through her, telling her to move away from him at once.

"Yes, it is." The gentleman chuckled and swayed again, his hand still reaching out to catch hers. "I am the most jovial of all the gentlemen in London! And, I confess, the most delightful. Every young lady in London wishes to be in my company so you are very favored indeed!"

Disliking the way the gentleman's eyes glittered, Prudence made to step back from him, only to bump into the wall of the ballroom. Panic began to climb up her throat as the gentleman advanced towards her, a clear desire set in his eyes.

"Now that you are in my company – and in such a private setting, I might add – is there something that you should like to garner from me? That *is* why we are here, is it not?"

Prudence's heart began to beat a little more furiously and she quickly shook her head. Clearly, this gentleman had drunk so much liquor that he had forgotten that he had come here of his own accord and had not made any plans whatsoever with her.

"You must be mistaking me for someone else, Lord...?"

She had hoped that the question would give him pause, that he would realize that she was not who he believed her to be, but the gentleman only grinned.

"Ah, you are playing a little coy with me now, are you not?" Laughing, he set one hand flat against the wall by her shoulder, his body now blocking her path to escape. "You need not tease me, Miss Villiers. I am sure that–"

"I am *not* Miss Villiers!" The fright that began to tear through her forced Prudence to act. She pressed one hand flat against the gentleman's chest as she spoke, seeing the grin on his face begin to fade as he looked down into her eyes. "You are mistaken. You are so much in your cups that you do not know where it is you are and who it is you are speaking to!"

"I believe that Miss Villiers is on the opposite side of the ballroom, Lord Childers."

Another voice came from behind Lord Childers and Prudence felt herself sag back against the wall just a little as the gentleman lifted his hand, turning to look at the person speaking.

"Is she?" he asked, looking to Prudence and then back to the other young lady who had spoken. "I thought that she..." With a frown, he turned and looked back into Prudence's face again before throwing up his hands and taking a step back. "Wait a moment! You are not Miss Villiers! Why are you pretending to be her?"

Prudence blinked furiously, her heart pounding with sudden frustration.

"I am *not* pretending to be this Miss Villiers! It is *you* who has chosen to come and confront me in this manner, believing that I am she."

The gentleman scowled.

"It is most unfair of you to pretend to be the lady I love," he said, his words still slurred at the edges. "Excuse me."

Before Prudence could protest, or even defend herself again, Lord Childers turned and walked away from them, though his steps were still a little wobbly. Letting out a harsh breath, Prudence pushed herself away from the wall just a little and then shook her head.

"I believe that Lord Childers has imbibed a great deal this evening," the young lady said, reminding Prudence that she was there. "I do hope that you are all right?"

"I am." Silently demanding that she pull her gaze away from the retreating figure of Lord Childers, Prudence eventually managed to look at the young lady who had saved her from his drunken advances. "I must thank you for what you did. If you had not come, then I am quite certain that he would have done something foolish."

"Yes," came the reply, a small, wry smile on the lips of the fair-haired lady, "especially if he believed you to be Miss Villiers." She winced, perhaps seeing the confusion in Prudence's expression. "Miss Villiers is known for her... interest... in the gentlemen of London."

Heat blossomed in Prudence's chest.

"I see."

"And he believed you to be her," the young lady continued, with a shrug. "You are rather similar with your dark hair and green eyes but that is all. You are a little taller than she, I think."

"And I certainly would not encourage him to come towards me in such an obvious and improper way." Not wanting this young lady to believe that she had done anything to encourage the gentleman's attentions, Prudence managed a faint smile. "That was rather shocking."

"I am certain it was, though I am glad he has done as I suggested." The young lady's smile grew wry. "Being in his cups means that he is very open to suggestion, it seems."

"Indeed." Recalling that she was still a wallflower and was generally ignored by society, Prudence smiled at the young lady. "Might I ask your name?"

The lady smiled.

"Of course, I should have done that at the beginning of this conversation." She bobbed her head. "I am Miss Anna Rockwell. My father is Viscount Drakewater."

"How very good to meet you." Prudence bobbed a curtsey. "I am Lady Prudence Twyford. My father is the Earl of Lymington." This, much to her relief, did not bring any sort of interest from Miss Rockwell, for her eyes did not flash with a sudden understanding, nor did she nod as though she recognized the name. Instead, she simply smiled. "It is a little unusual to have a lady such as yourself standing back here," Prudence continued, not wanting Miss Rockwell to ask the question before she did. "Were you following Lord Childers for some reason?"

Miss Rockwell laughed and shook her head.

"No, indeed not. I am betrothed, you see – though not to Lord Childers – and my betrothed is currently absent from London. Given that I have no interest in any other gentleman aside from him, I find there to be very little point in attending occasions such as these. My mother insists, however, for we are to keep up our appearances here in London so that the *ton* knows all is well."

Prudence smiled sympathetically.

"I can imagine that must be something of a trial for you. Might I ask where your betrothed is at present?"

Miss Rockwell sighed and shook her head.

"Business forced him to return to his estate - business which he simply could not put off. It seems that his sister and her husband have had some financial difficulties of late – not of their own doing. The crops have done very badly, and a lot of the interests that... well, that does not matter." She shrugged. "Needless to say, Lord Yates decided to return to his estate to make certain that all was going as he expected, though he intends to be of aid to his brother-in-law, I believe."

"That is very generous of him."

Miss Rockwell smiled softly, her eyes holding a gentleness that spoke of a true affection for her betrothed.

"He is a very generous man." For a moment, nothing more was said, only for Miss Rockwell to give herself a slight shake and then look back at Prudence with interest. "And you? Why are you hiding here, might I ask?"

Prudence hesitated. She wanted to suggest that it was a little bold to ask such a question when they were only just introduced but, given that she herself had asked such a thing, it was not as though she could.

"Society has decided that I am to be a wallflower," she said eventually, not giving any further explanation than that. "My parents are encouraging me to step forward as it is a new Season now since they decided that I am to be pushed back in such a way, but I have not yet found the confidence to do such a thing."

Miss Rockwell nodded, turning to look out across the room rather than holding Prudence's gaze.

"It can be difficult," she agreed, softly, "but I would encourage you to step out. If you have the opportunity, why should you not?"

Prudence pulled her mouth to one side.

"I am afraid of what they will do," she said, finding her heart filled with a desire to unburden herself. If she told Miss Rockwell the truth, then she could decide whether or not she wanted to linger in Prudence's company. And if she did not, then Prudence would be left alone again, just as she had anticipated. "You see, Miss Rockwell, I was discovered in a room with a gentleman. This gentleman was in his cups and... well, I was present with him. It did not end in matrimony for various reasons, but society has not taken well to such a thing."

Miss Rockwell turned her head and looked back at Prudence steadily for some moments. Prudence's stomach twisted this way and that, heat beginning to spread up her spine and into her shoulders, her heart beginning to quicken furiously. What would Miss Rockwell say to such a thing? Was she going to bid Prudence good evening and step away? Prudence could not blame her if she did. There was enough of the truth there to keep all of the *ton* from her.

"Lady Prudence." Miss Rockwell smiled, her expression gentling. "You need not think that I will remove myself from your company because of any past experiences or situations you might have suffered. I can see that you might be in need of a friend which, I must admit, is something that I am also seeking." With a small tilt of her head, she shrugged her shoulders lightly. "What say you, Lady Prudence? Might you be willing to be my friend this Season?"

Prudence blinked, tears beginning to build behind her eyes as her throat tightened. This young lady had no knowledge of Prudence's past, had no real understanding of who she was, yet she was willing to step into a friendship with her, should Prudence be willing. Part of her wanted to confess everything to Miss Rockwell, to tell her all that she had done and how much of a fool she had been, but the other part of her held that back. Miss Rockwell had only just stated that she did not care about the past and therefore, Prudence was not going to torment herself with such things either.

"That is an offer I could not even think to refuse," Prudence answered, seeing how the broad smile spread right across Miss Rockwell's face. "Thank you, Miss Rockwell. I feel a good deal better already, knowing that I now have company!"

"As do I." Miss Rockwell let out a small, contented sigh and then came to stand beside Prudence, looking out at the ballroom. "This has turned out to be a rather pleasing evening after all!"

Prudence nodded, the tension within her frame beginning to untwist and fade away for what was the first time since she had set foot into the ballroom.

"Yes, Miss Rockwell," she agreed, smiling. "It certainly has been."

CHAPTER TWO

"You are too much in your cups to dance!"

James laughed and rolled his eyes.

"I certainly am not!" He stood tall, not swaying an inch. "I may have imbibed a little too much at the ball yesterday evening, but I am quite determined not to be so overcome again."

His friend narrowed his eyes at him, though there was still a playful lilt about his mouth.

"I am sure that I saw you with a glass of brandy only a few minutes ago."

"Mayhap you did, but I set it down," James told him, seeing his friend grin. "I certainly did *not* throw it back!"

This had them both laughing aloud, each knowing full well that James would never have done such a foolish thing as to leave a glass of brandy unattended! That was what the Season was for, was it not? It was a chance to do just as he pleased, to eat, to drink, and to make as much merriment as he could. He had enjoyed many a Season thus far and yet, still, he had not grown tired of it.

"I am still not certain that you should dance," Lord Kingshill stated, folding his arms across his chest though he continued to grin all the same. "There are too many young ladies present who could find themselves injured by your foolishness! And you have a reputation to think of."

James snorted.

"Ah yes, my *pristine* reputation which I must keep hold of," he answered, making Lord Kingshill laugh. "Come now, you know as well as I that I have no intention of worrying about such things this Season."

"Nor next year, no doubt," Lord Kingshill chuckled. "When the time comes for us both to find a bride, I am not certain that either of us will be able to do so! Our reputations will be so terribly damaged that even the wallflowers will reject us!"

Considering this for a moment, James shrugged.

"I have no concerns. When I offer my hand to some young lady, I have no doubt that she will accept. The same could be said for you, for you have just as high a title as I, though I have a good deal more coin than you."

Lord Kingshill's eyes flared.

"Is that so?" he asked, shoving James backward, making him laugh. "I think you are a little too bold – or mayhap a little too prideful – there, my friend."

Knowing Lord Kingshill was only mocking, James did not take offense.

"Mayhap I am," he grinned, "though what I am doing my utmost to express is that *you,* the Marquess of Kingshill, only has to look at a young lady for her to smile back at you with big, bright eyes."

"Until their father or mother realizes who I am and pulls her back from me," Lord Kingshill muttered, his good humor evaporating. "Mayhap I *should* be thinking a little more about my reputation this Season."

Feeling suddenly alarmed, James' eyes grew wide, and he took a step closer, putting his hand on Lord Kingshill's shoulder.

"You are concerned about nothing," he said, firmly. "I assure you that your title, your good fortune, and your large estate will do you very well when the time comes to seek a bride."

Lord Kingshill shook his head.

"No, I do not think so." He ran one hand through his hair and, letting out a long, slow breath, turned his head away to look out across the ballroom. "I have never thought about such a thing before, but now that you have said such things, I find that I am a little concerned. I am well aware of my responsibilities, now that I have taken on the title, but the last two Seasons, I have chosen to deliberately forget them."

"That is not true," James interjected, speaking as firmly as he dared. "You have always managed your estate well. Your finances are excellent, and the investments you have made have proven to be more than satisfactory."

"But that does not detract from the fact that I have not considered my future, nor the requirement to produce an heir." Lord Kingshill shook his head again, his expression tight. "I have only a sister, so if something should happen to me, then my family line will pass to some distant relation!" His shoulders dropped. "I have not been thinking seriously about such things at all. Now, mayhap, I ought to be doing so."

Feeling himself a little panicked now, frightened that his friend was being so quickly pulled into this deep way of thinking, James tried to find something to say that would encourage him *not* to go on considering his present situation, but nothing came to mind. Instead, he closed his eyes and frowned, waiting for clarity to come to him.

"It is not something that you need to rush into," he said, eventually. "There is no requirement for you to be hasty in this, I assure you. You are being much too severe and—"

"No, Childers." Lord Kingshill turned quickly, one hand slicing through the air between them, his eyes sharp now. "No. For the first time, I have been thinking clearly. It has come upon me rather unexpectedly, certainly, but I see now that I cannot continue as I have been. It was foolishness of me to think that I could do so."

In an instant, all that James had thought of for the upcoming Season, all he had considered that might be, went up like smoke. He was not going to have his companion with him, was not going to be able to pursue nothing but laughter and pleasure in the same way that he had done previously. Somehow, without having any intention of doing so, James had managed to speak into Lord Kingshill's conscience and now, it seemed, his friend was going to behave very differently this Season.

"I shall have to find a suitable young lady." Lord Kingshill raked one hand through his hair and let out a hiss of breath. "I am suspicious that it shall be very difficult indeed to do such a thing. The *ton* is well aware of my reputation as a rake! They think me nothing but a scoundrel, so how shall I ever find a young lady who will think well of me?"

"Does such a thing matter?" Giving up on the idea of pulling such thoughts from Lord Kingshill, James shrugged his shoulders as his friend scowled. "You can make an arrangement with a young lady's father and, thereafter, proceed into marriage without having any sort of courtship or the like. The young lady herself need not even agree to wed you! So long as her father is contented, the arrangement can be made and all will be well."

Lord Kingshill rubbed his chin.

"I suppose that is one consideration."

"*And*," James continued, finding himself a little less concerned now that Lord Kingshill had agreed to his previous statement, "once that is done and the arrangement made, you can continue on just as you please! You need not be a devoted suitor, not if it is an arranged match. After all, it is not as though you are going to care for the lady, is it?"

His friend turned to him and, after a moment, began to nod.

"I can see the wisdom in what you are saying. Heaven knows that I do not want to become a very staid, dull fellow who only thinks of his wife and *her* requirements!"

"You could even leave your wife back at your estate during future Seasons!" James exclaimed, warming to the conversation now that his friend appeared to be a little less concerned. "That way, you will be free of her for a few months and can continue with all that you enjoy."

Lord Kingshill nodded and, after a moment, offered James a small, wry smile.

"I think you are more concerned about your own lack of company than my enjoyment of whatever situation I find myself in!"

James laughed, though a flicker of embarrassment entered his heart.

"Mayhap some of that is true, though I am truly concerned for your welfare," he promised, as Lord Kingshill chuckled. "You do not believe me, I understand, though it is quite true. I do not want you to become a frustrated, ill-tempered fellow who is no longer able to do as he pleases! Find yourself a match, arrange it with the lady's father, and thereafter, return to all that you enjoy."

"I think I shall."

"And I shall help you, of course," James said quickly, the desire to do such a thing coming solely from his intentions for an enjoyable Season alongside his closest friend. Once the arrangement was made, once Lord Kingshill was betrothed, both he and James himself could return to simply enjoying the Season and to the roguish reputations that they both enjoyed.

"Well, I thank you." Lord Kingshill scowled, his expression dark. "I do not want to do such a thing but now that I see the situation clearly, I think that I must. Though all the same, I do think that it will be rather difficult to find a young lady to betrothe myself to without courtship and the like. They will all expect such a thing, and I do not have the desire, nor the inclination, for such things."

"Then find a young lady who will accept you without

the requirement for courtship! Find someone who will be quite willing to accept your hand, for she will have no other options available to her."

Lord Kingshill frowned.

"What do you mean? You wish me to marry someone impoverished? Someone who is well below my title of Marquess? While I understand where such a thought comes from, I have no desire to marry the daughter of a Baronet or a Knight! I would not demean myself in that way."

James shook his head.

"No, that is not what I mean. Why do you not find a wallflower?" He watched as the idea brought the light of understanding to Lord Kingshill's face. "You see what I mean? There will be a reason behind each wallflower's presence, of course, but so long as it is not entirely disagreeable, there is no reason not to pursue such a young lady. She will have no other gentlemen pursuing her, and will be very glad to accept you – as will her father, whoever he may be, I am sure."

It was with relief that he watched Lord Kingshill begin to nod slowly, rubbing one hand over his chin.

"A wallflower," Lord Kingshill mused aloud. "Yes, I see that such a young lady might be more than suitable for my requirements."

"And would agree to it all very quickly," James interjected. "You could find yourself betrothed by the end of the sennight, should you wish it!"

Lord Kingshill chuckled, flinging his hands out.

"Then what is it that we are waiting for? Come! Let us go in search of a wallflower at this very moment!"

With a chuckle, James followed his friend, relief surging through him. This conversation had been most unexpected, but James was sure that it would be resolved very quickly indeed. His friend would secure himself a betrothal, the wedding date would be set, and then both he and Lord Kingshill could enjoy the rest of the Season, just as they had always planned.

CHAPTER THREE

*P*rudence let a slow smile spread across her face as she walked through the beautiful gardens of St James' Park. Her father and mother were only a short distance ahead of her and, though she had walked with them both for a time, she had stepped back once her mother had begun wondering aloud about what sort of gentleman might be willing to even *consider* Prudence's hand.

That had been difficult to hear and, though her father had quietened the conversation quickly, it had been enough to set Prudence back from them both for a time. She was all too aware of just how difficult it would be to find her match. The problem with the *ton* was that they had long memories, and a deep unwillingness to forgive - which meant that, no matter where she went or what she did, someone would recall who she was and what she had done. There would be a whisper about her, someone talking out of the corner of their mouth to another, and Prudence would feel that creeping sense of upset and mortification, shame beginning to bite down upon her heart again.

It had happened last evening when she had done her best to step out into society with her mother. The soiree had been small and intimate, and she had been pleased with the small smiles and the nods which she had been able to share with some of the other guests, but when she had tried to step into the conversation, she had caught the glances which had flicked between one lady and the next, leaving her in no doubt as to what they had been speaking about. No one had offered her any sort of conversation, no one had reached out to speak to her and she had simply stood there, silently. Her mother had continued the conversation for her. She had tried her best to bring Prudence into it, but none of the other guests had even the smallest bit of willingness to assist. They had ignored her and, in the end, Prudence had stepped back into the shadows and, despite her mother's cajoling, had refused to come out again.

Little wonder that my mother feels such despair over me and my prospects.

With a small sigh, the smile on Prudence's face crumpled as her heart dropped like a stone. She had no one to blame for this situation apart from herself, and though she felt as though she deserved every drop of censure, every disconcerting glance, the pain was heavy upon her.

"Lady Prudence!"

She turned her head, only to see someone waving at her from only a short distance away. Pausing, she smiled as Miss Rockwell hurried towards her, leaving someone behind her.

"Good afternoon, Miss Rockwell." Prudence gestured to her mother and father. "We are out walking in the park, as you see."

"As am I!" Miss Rockwell looked back over her shoulder. "My mother is coming after me now. Mayhap we should permit them to be introduced?"

Prudence nodded and, asking her parents to join them, quickly made the introductions. Miss Rockwell's mother was a very pleasant lady, with a warm smile and a kindness about her which Prudence recognized at once. It seemed that Miss Rockwell possessed the same tender-heartedness as her mother and, for that, Prudence found herself grateful. Lord and Lady Lymington and Lady Drakewater soon fell into conversation and Prudence and Miss Rockwell turned aside, choosing to have their own conversation rather than linger with their parents.

"A very pleasant afternoon, is it not?" Miss Rockwell smiled as they wandered together, making sure not to stray too far from their parents. "I have had a letter from my betrothed, so to me, it feels as though the sunshine is a little brighter and the air a little warmer than before!"

"That is good." Prudence looked at her friend. "And Lord Yates? How does he fare?"

The smile faded just a little from her friend's face.

"He is contented that things are going as they should be, though I confess that I am still a little disappointed."

"Oh?"

"He is not to come back to London," Miss Rockwell sighed, looking away from Prudence. "I thought that he would return soon, but it seems that I am to be held back from him for a little longer."

Prudence blinked in surprise at hearing the lady speaking with such obvious affection.

"You care for him, then?"

Miss Rockwell glanced up at her and then returned her gaze to the path.

"I know that it is most unusual for one to care for one's betrothed, but yes, my heart is certainly tender towards him. I think him an excellent gentleman, with a very kind and considerate heart and thus, I could not *help* but think well of him. Our letters have been very frequent and the words of affection within them have increased from both myself, *and* from him." She smiled, her face coloring just a little. "It seems a little strange to say that letters have improved our connection, but they have! I did not think that my heart would ever feel such a sweetness towards any gentleman, but Lord Yates has brought that about in me, simply by who he is." With a small, contented sigh, she tossed another glance to Prudence. "When it comes to making a match, I think a match where there is affection between husband and wife is the very best of marriages."

Prudence said nothing for a few minutes, letting the silence drift between them, though there was no awkwardness about it. She had never given any thought to finding affection when it came to making a match and, even now, she could not say that it was something which she truly desired.

"I have not even thought about such things," she admitted, eventually. "When I first thought about finding a suitable husband, I considered only title and fortune. Even now, that is all that I think about."

"Oh?" Miss Rockwell tilted her head so that she could look at Prudence a little better, her fair curls pushed back by the wind. "Do you believe that you would be truly contented with a husband who had no genuine consideration for you?"

Prudence nodded.

"Yes, I believe that I would."

"Well, I certainly would *not* be," came the reply. "I want nothing more than to have a husband who cares for me, who adores me, and who I can love in return. And with Lord Yates, it seems that I am to have it! It is such a blessing, I can hardly believe it!"

"I am glad for you," Prudence answered, honestly. "For myself, however, I believe that I will be glad for any match that I can get!" Her brow furrowed, and she cast a quick glance at a group of gentlemen whom they had just walked past. "Though even now, none of them so much as glance at me."

"No doubt that is because they are talking of nothing but gambling and horses, and are paying no attention to *anyone* who walks past here," Miss Rockwell said, making Prudence smile rather ruefully. "It is not simply because you are a wallflower, I assure you."

"Ho, there!"

Hearing something behind her, Prudence glanced over her shoulder, only for her heart to quicken in astonishment. A gentleman was hurrying after them, waving one hand as though he were attempting to catch their attention. Turning her head back to the path and presuming that whoever this gentleman was waving at was ahead of them, Prudence found herself all the more confused, given that there was nobody there.

"If you would but give me a few moments of your time?"

Prudence glanced at Miss Rockwell.

"Is this fellow speaking to us?"

Miss Rockwell glanced over her shoulder and then, after a moment, nodded.

"I believe so."

"Are you acquainted with him?"

"No," came the answer, "but from his broad smile, it seems that we soon shall be!"

Prudence hesitated, aware that they had not been formally introduced. Having no desire to bring any sort of further shame upon herself, she took Miss Rockwell's arm.

"Might we be cautious, Miss Rockwell? I do not want society to think worse of me than they do already!"

Miss Rockwell nodded and, unable to ignore the calls of the gentleman any longer, Prudence turned around directly, keeping her chin lifted as the gentleman approached. He smiled and inclined his head, beaming at her as though they had already been introduced and he was now delighted to see her again. Prudence did not recognize his face – handsome though he was – and, with another curious glance towards Miss Rockwell, she waited for the gentleman to introduce himself.

Much to her astonishment, he did not.

"Might I ask if I heard you correctly?"

Caught all the more by astonishment, it took Prudence a moment to answer. Instead of answering his question, however, she arched one eyebrow and kept her head held high.

"Might I ask if we have been introduced?"

The gentleman paused for a moment and then, much to Prudence's surprise, laughed jovially as though she had said something mirthful, his brown eyes twinkling.

"Very good, very good," he said, then wiggling his finger at her as if she were still a child who was being lectured by her schoolmistress. "But I must beg to know whether you were speaking honestly or not."

"Whether we were or not, it does not give you the right to simply demand to know such things from us!" Miss Rockwell broke in, her eyes flashing with clear anger. "Goodness, I do not think that I have ever come across a gentleman who would speak in such a manner!"

The gentleman looked at Miss Rockwell for a moment before, much to her surprise, he dropped into a bow and, upon rising, kept his head lowered as his dark hair fell forward over his forehead.

"I am truly sorry," he said, sounding rather contrite though Prudence was still quite uncertain of him, not sure what he was about. "There is a situation which I am doing my best to resolve and, hearing what was said between you has filled me with all manner of hope and expectation!"

Prudence looked at Miss Rockwell, who merely offered her a slight shrug, telling her silently that it was up to her whether they stayed to listen to him or not. A little afraid that this gentleman would call after her and embarrass her all the more if she walked away, Prudence chose to remain where she was, looking back at the fellow as he finally met her gaze.

Something rippled over her, but she ignored it, giving herself a slight shake to remove it from herself. This gentleman, whoever he was, had a handsomeness about him; a small, lilting smile that was a little coy, brown eyes that were warm and hopeful, and a strength to his frame which was obvious simply in the way that he moved. Prudence pushed such thoughts aside, however, and with what she hoped was an obvious sigh, put out her hands to either side in question.

"Might we know your title, my Lord? At least that way, though we are not formally introduced as we ought to be, we will not be speaking to a stranger."

He grinned at her, the light in his eyes sending another ripple of that odd sensation over her skin, but Prudence did not react, other than to gaze back at him with a steady gaze.

"Wonderful," he said, bowing for what was now the second time. "I am the Marquess of Childers."

Prudence blinked in surprise, a little astonished that a Marquess would come to speak to them without being properly introduced first. Was not he a gentleman who knew the rules of propriety? Or was this matter at hand so urgent that he could not hold himself back, as he had said?

"Miss Rockwell and Lady Prudence," Miss Rockwell stated, not going into detail with her introduction as regards who their fathers were and the like. "Now, what was the purpose of your demand that we stop and listen to you?"

As Prudence watched, Lord Childers turned his eyes towards *her*, no longer looking at Miss Rockwell, but rather fixing all of his attention upon her. She shivered lightly, a little uncertain about what such an intense look might mean, finding herself stepping back when he moved only a little closer.

"Lady Prudence," he said, his voice softer now, as though he were attempting to cajole her into something. "Daughter of...?"

She frowned.

"My father is the Earl of Lymington."

Lord Childers rubbed his hands, his grin returning.

"Capital!" he exclaimed, his exuberance as yet unexplained. "The daughter of an Earl, then! Wonderful."

Becoming all the more confused and unsettled by his exclamations, Prudence forced herself to step forward and, glaring at Lord Childers, folded her arms over her chest.

"Explain yourself, Lord Childers, or we shall take our leave within the moment," she said, a little harshly. "I will not wait any longer for your explanation."

"Of course, of course." Dropping his hands to his sides again, he beamed at her. "I overheard you saying that you would be glad to make a match with anyone. Might I be bold enough to ask if such words were genuine?"

A furious heat enveloped Prudence as she stared at the gentleman, her whole body feeling heavy and weighted. Beside her, Miss Rockwell began to splutter with indignation, telling Lord Childers exactly what it was that she thought of his question, though Lord

Childers himself did not look anywhere but at Prudence's face, waiting for her to respond.

Prudence closed her eyes for a few moments, mortification sweeping through her. She had not thought for a moment that anyone had overheard her speaking in such a way, and to know that this gentleman had done so filled her with nothing other than shame and embarrassment.

"Do not be afraid to tell me," Lord Childers told her, ignoring Miss Rockwell's exclamations and speaking only to Prudence. "There is a purpose in my question."

"And what might that be?" Prudence asked, a little hoarsely, her face burning with heat. "What possible reason could a gentleman such as yourself have in asking me such a thing?"

Again, that seemingly ever-ready smile returned to Lord Childers' face as he moved a fraction closer to her.

"Why, Lady Prudence," he began, softly, "it is because I believe that I have a match for you."

CHAPTER FOUR

"*Y*ou did *what?*"

James spread out his hands as he and Lord Kingshill sat together in James' drawing room.

"I did what I thought was best. I could not let such a young lady escape, could I?"

Lord Kingshill shook his head and groaned aloud.

"When you said that you would be of aid to me in this situation, I did not think that it meant you would go out to *find* a young lady on my behalf."

"I did not find her," James clarified, finding himself a little frustrated that his friend was not reacting with any sort of delight, or even interest, to what James had discovered. "She walked past me, and I overheard her saying something about being glad for any match she might be given and, on hearing that, I pursued her to discover whether or not that statement was true, and not made flippantly." Lord Kingshill picked up his glass of brandy from the table and took a long draught, saying nothing though, James noted, he still did not look in the least bit pleased. "She is eager for a match," he continued, wondering why Lord Kingshill was frowning. "It was something of a strange conversation, of course, for she did not know who I was or why I was asking such a thing, but I was glad to speak with her about your circumstances all the same."

Lord Kingshill blinked.

"You told her of what I said?"

"I told her only that you were also seeking a match – and perhaps, even a hasty one – though I reassured her that there was no dark or dangerous reason for that." Chuckling, though the tension still raked over him, James shrugged his shoulders. "I did not think that there was anything wrong in what I said. I do hope that you are not troubled in some way."

"Not troubled, no," came the slow reply, as Lord Kingshill looked at him thoughtfully. "Though I confess that I am rather surprised that you would think to speak to this young lady in such a way, without my agreement."

"Oh." James hesitated, his eyebrows drawing together. "My dear friend, I did not think that there was any such thing required from you. You had already accepted my offer of help and–"

"Yes, but that did not mean that I had granted you permission to tell any young lady you pleased about my decision and my requirements!" Lord Kingshill exclaimed, his face coloring just a little. "No doubt she is now going about London, telling all and sundry about this strange gentleman who has come up to her and, on his friend's behalf, practically offering her a betrothal!"

James shook his head.

"I did no such thing, and it is not as severe as you might think," he said, firmly. "First of all, I did not tell the young lady your name, nor did I ever once suggest that you and she might become betrothed. All I said was that I had a friend who was looking for a suitable match and might very well be interested in courting her."

His shoulders lifted, though his spirits dropped, having expected his friend to be delighted with all that James had done.

Lord Kingshill threw back the rest of his brandy and then shook his head.

"It is all a little unexpected." He shot James a side-long glance. "Though I must say, now that I consider it, I suppose that I should feel some gratitude."

A little relieved, James managed to smile.

"It would be appreciated, yes. I–"

"I should ask," Lord Kingshill interrupted, before James had even finished speaking, "is there some reason that this young lady has not found a suitable match as yet?" His eyes suddenly flared wide. "Is it because she is ugly? Is she dreadfully plain?"

Considering for a moment, James was quick to reassure his friend.

"No, indeed not. I think, if I am to be honest, that she is very lovely indeed."

"Oh?"

James nodded, bringing the young Lady Prudence to mind. "She is lovely, with a gentle figure, a softness about her lips, vivid green eyes that remind me of the great oak's leaves on a fine summer's day, and brown hair which – "

"Which reminds you of the trunk of said oak tree?" Lord Kingshill interrupted though, this time, much to James' relief, there was a quirk to his lips. "You do not have to paint a very fine picture of this lady, my friend. I believe you. If you say that she is not plain, then she is not plain. She will be pretty enough for me." He reached for his brandy glass, only to seem to recall that it was empty, and set it down on the table beside them with a scowl darkening his features. "I shall ask again, however, what it is that has prevented her from making a match thus far?" As he spoke, his expression grew serious all over again. "There must be some reason that a young lady of the *ton* has not made a betrothal as yet, especially if this is not her first Season."

He looked at James with a slightly lifted eyebrow and James nodded.

"I presume it is not. She certainly does not seem a green girl."

"A spinster then?"

James shook his head.

"No, not yet, though mayhap that will come soon should she not find a suitable match."

"Which is why she is now willing to marry anyone she can," Lord Kingshill finished for James, who smiled his relief at his friend's understanding.

"Yes, precisely." James tilted his head. "*And* she is the daughter of an Earl. So it is no great step down for you either!"

Slowly, Lord Kingshill began to nod, and James' hopes began to rise.

"So she is not plain, there is nothing untoward about her, and she has no dreadful rumors pinned to her name."

Inwardly, James hesitated though, outwardly, he shook his head.

"No, of course not."

That was one thing he had not thought about, he realized. He had not wondered if there was a reason *why* this particular lady was a spinster. She was pretty enough and, as he had just said to Lord Kingshill, the daughter of an Earl. So why *was* she a spinster?

I shall resolve to find out, James decided, as his friend began to consider aloud as to whether it would be wise to pursue this particular lady. *Though, even if there are rumors or gossip or the like, it is not as though Lord Kingshill has a perfect reputation!*

"Will you introduce me to her, then?"

James looked back to his friend, nodding fervently.

"Yes, of course. This evening? I am sure that she will be at Lord Frederickson's ball."

For the first time since the beginning of their conversation, Lord Kingshill smiled broadly, then slapped his knee with the palm of his hand.

"Excellent! Do you know, I am suddenly looking forward to this evening!"

Chuckling, James got up and went to refill Lord Kingshill's brandy glass, as well as his own.

"Excellent. The sooner you are betrothed, the sooner we can return to enjoying this London Season... and all the other ones that will follow!"

"Lady Prudence, there you are." Ignoring the startled look which spread across the young lady's face, James cleared his throat and then bowed his head briefly, by way of greeting. "We must speak."

Lady Prudence blinked.

"I – good evening, Lord Childers." She bobbed a quick curtsey. "As you can see, you have caught me a little by surprise. I am soon expecting Miss Rockwell and–"

"That is not important. What I must ask you is–"

"Lord Childers!"

James came to a stop, looking back into Lady Prudence's eyes and finding himself rather astonished at the fierce expression that had crossed her face. Not only had she interrupted him, but she was now narrowing her eyes at him, as though he were somehow in the wrong. Her cheeks were a little flushed and, as he looked at her, she folded her arms across her chest and then set her jaw.

"Have I done something to offend you?" he asked, speaking a good deal more slowly now, trying to understand the reason for her upset.

"Yes, you have." Lady Prudence lifted her chin a notch and kept her narrowed gaze fixed to his. "You may well think that I, being a wallflower, will be more than contented to have you come to speak to me in such a forward manner, when I have no other company with me and am entirely alone, but I assure you, I am not. In case you have forgotten about the required propriety in this sort of situation, might I remind you that no gentleman

should be found speaking to a lady when she is unchaper-
oned. I would appreciate it if you would show me a little
more consideration."

Still somewhat astonished by the audacity with
which she spoke, it took James some moments to respond.
He had not thought for a moment about propriety. Why
should he? He had never had cause to do so, and certainly
did not think to do so now. But if he refused, he considered, then Lady Prudence would not be at all willing to
listen to him, and the potential arrangement between
herself and Lord Kingshill might fail entirely.

James swallowed his pride and inclined his head.

"Of course. Forgive me." His hands clenched hard as
he bit back the question ringing around in his head -
namely, why someone who was nothing more than a wallflower should have any concern over propriety! It was not
as though society paid her the least bit of attention. "I
shall wait until Miss Rockwell has joined you," he added,
taking a step back and then watching as she turned
herself a little away from him, making it quite clear that
they were no longer in conversation.

As he waited, James found himself considering the
lady, watching her carefully, taking in her profile. She
was, he considered, a little more than *pretty*, even though
that was what he had said to Lord Kingshill. There was
the gentle slope of her neck, the softness about her
expression, her high cheeks, rosebud lips, and long,
copper tresses that had been pulled to the top of her
head and fell all the way to her shoulders. Absently,
James found himself wondering just how long the lady's
hair might be once all the pins had been removed and

just how soft it might feel, should he run his hands through it.

That thought stopped him short and he froze in place, his eyes still fixed to the lady. Whatever was he doing? He could not let himself think such things or even have any sort of interest in Lady Prudence, not if he was to place her beside Lord Kingshill! That would be disastrous for, as much as both he and Lord Kingshill were rogues, James knew for certain that Lord Kingshill would never even *consider* a lady whom James had previously held in his arms. Finding himself lost in his thoughts, James ran one hand over his chin, trying to remind himself to think practically about it all, only to sense a pair of eyes resting on him.

He frowned, straightened, and then saw Miss Rockwell and Lady Prudence standing together and looking at him, though there was still a sharpness in Lady Prudence's gaze, and a heavy frown pulling at Miss Rockwell's expression. Clearly, neither lady thought well of him.

"Good evening." Recalling that Lady Prudence expected propriety, James bowed his head, first to Lady Prudence and then to Miss Rockwell. "I wonder, Lady Prudence, if I might speak with you for a moment?"

Lady Prudence's expression did not change.

"You wish to introduce me to your friend, yes?"

"Yes, I do. You have not refused to consider the idea and so I thought that this evening, I might make the introductions. He is eager to meet you."

The two ladies shared a glance, though James could not see into it to understand what it meant. Lady

Prudence bit her lip and then, after a moment, sighed and shook her head.

"I do not know whether this is a wise thought, Lord Childers. You have not yet told me the name of this gentleman friend of yours, nor why he is so urgent in his desire to marry."

James opened his mouth to explain, only to then frown and look away. There would be no purpose in revealing all of this to her if there was some dark reason behind her situation on why she was ,a wallflower. "Might I ask, Lady Prudence, if–"

"Good evening."

Before James could finish his sentence, an older lady – whom he presumed was mother to one of the ladies – came to stand between them. She shot a look towards James and then turned to Lady Prudence.

"Mama, are you acquainted with Lord Childers?"

The moment Lady Prudence said his name, James saw the recognition ripple across her mother's face. There was a pause and then, after a moment, the lady turned to look at James, a coolness in her expression.

"I am not acquainted with him, but I know of him, yes," came the reply, though Lady Prudence did not appear to notice this coldness, quickly making the introductions. James bowed and then straightened, a hint of panic beginning to course through him. If Lady Lymington refused to let her daughter speak further with him, then the plan in its entirety would fall to the ground and shatter into a thousand pieces.

I cannot let that happen.

"Might I ask what a gentleman such as yourself is

doing speaking with my daughter?" Lady Lymington asked, ice now shining in her eyes. "And at the back of the ballroom too?"

James put out his hands, attempting to demonstrate that he had no ill intent. "I came only to speak with both Lady Prudence and Miss Rockwell," he said, aware that Lady Lymington might consider him something of a threat to her daughter's reputation. "And now, in fact, I came to see if either of them wished to stand up to dance."

In a moment, everything changed. Lady Lymington blinked, her eyes then flared and she turned to her daughter, who was staring at James in sheer astonishment. With a quiet cough, James dropped his hands before looking to Miss Rockwell and then back to Lady Prudence.

"Well?" he asked, forcing a smile onto his face which he did not truly feel. "Shall I have the pleasure of standing up with either of you this evening? I should be truly honored to do so."

CHAPTER FIVE

*P*rudence did not understand what it was that Lord Childers was doing in offering her such a thing. To stand and talk openly with a wallflower was one thing, but to dance with her was quite another! Her heart quickened into a furious, wild rhythm, encouraging her to pull her dance card from her wrist and hand it to him, but one glance into her mother's face held her back.

"You wish to dance with myself and Lady Prudence?" Miss Rockwell shook her head. "I am afraid that I shall have to decline. I have made a promise to myself that I shall dance with no other gentlemen until my betrothed is returned to me."

"How very honorable," came the reply, though Lord Childers brown eyes soon swept back towards Prudence, making her skin prickle with sudden anticipation. "Then you, Lady Prudence? Might you be willing to stand up with me?"

Prudence did not know what to say. This had not been his real purpose in coming to speak with her, that she knew for certain. Mayhap, she considered, the presence of her mother had forced him to come up with an excuse – and this was the only one he could give her.

"Prudence, Lord Childers is a rogue." Prudence started in surprise at just how loud and clear her mother's voice was, her face heating furiously at just how boldly she spoke. "I will not forbid you from dancing with him, but I shall also make it quite plain that I shall be watching every step of the dance." Lady Lymington turned to face Lord Childers, and Prudence, her face still burning, dropped her gaze. "Lord Childers, I do not know what your intentions are for my daughter, nor what your purpose is in seeking her out, but I will *not* have you ruining her reputation."

Lord Childers nodded.

"I can understand your uncertainty over my presence, Lady Lymington. However, let me state that I have absolutely no intention of doing anything other than dance with Lady Prudence. I shall return her to you thereafter, I promise you."

Prudence wanted to say that she had not yet given him her dance card and had not even agreed to do so but, after a moment's pause, found her fingers tugging the ribbon from her wrist and, without daring to glance at her mother, she handed the dance card to him.

I have not danced for so long, she thought to herself, a sudden burst of joy exploding in her heart. *How wonderful that shall be, even if I am accompanied by a rogue!*

"The country dance, Lady Prudence?" Lord Childers smiled and then handed it back to her. "I shall come to find you for the dance, when it is time." He bowed and then smiled. "Good evening."

"Good evening," Prudence echoed, watching him walk away and, after only a few moments, hearing her mother's long, drawn-out sigh of evident frustration.

"That gentleman is not to be trusted, Prudence." Lady Lymington turned so that she might look straight into Prudence's eyes, her gaze steady, but her eyes holding flickers of worry. "I do not know what he thought to do by coming to speak with you, but I must have you promise me that you will not allow yourself to be drawn in to whatever scheme he has planned."

Prudence nodded.

"Of course, Mama, though I do not think that he has a scheme."

"Rogues like that always have a scheme," came the reply, her mother finally letting go of her hands. "I am doing my best to protect you, my dear, and Lord Childers is someone you must be protected *from*."

"I understand." Prudence chose not to argue, aware that *she* knew the reason behind Lord Childers supposed interest in her, while her mother did not. "I will be very careful, Mama."

Lady Lymington nodded but said nothing more, her gaze returning to the retreating figure of Lord Childers and, after a moment, Prudence let herself watch him too. He was a handsome gentleman, she had to admit, with a charming smile, warm brown eyes, and a pleasantness about his manner that could make any young lady – Prudence included – fall for his charms, should she let herself do so.

But I will not, she told herself, a little perturbed that he should be known as something of a rogue. *And I must pray that his friend, whoever that gentleman may be, will not turn out to be just as much of a scoundrel as Lord Childers!*

"ARE YOU ENJOYING THE DANCE, Lady Prudence?"

Prudence took a moment to reply, stepping away from him for a time as the dance progressed only to return to his side once more.

"Yes, I am," she said, aware that the rest of the *ton* would have taken note of a wallflower stepping out with a rogue, finding herself a little concerned that their interaction would cause her reputation to be all the more damaged. "But I assume, Lord Childers, that you did not want truly to dance with me, did you? There was another reason for stepping out with me, was there not?"

Lord Childers grinned.

"Indeed, there was." The smile began to fade as a frown slowly began to cross his forehead. "I must ask you why you are a wallflower."

The shock of his question had Prudence stumbling, though he quickly caught her back into his arms and the dance continued. He did not apologize for what he had said, however, waiting for her to answer.

"Why are you asking me such a thing?" Prudence asked, a little breathless from her astonishment rather than from the dance. "What could possibly push you to ask me such a question as this?"

Lord Childers' eyebrows lifted just a little.

"Surely you can understand, Lady Prudence? My friend, the one I am to introduce you to tonight, is a little concerned to know if there is a reason behind your standing as a wallflower. Obviously, it is important to him, as a gentleman of quality, that he is pursuing a young lady who has no dark shadows in her past."

Prudence lifted her chin, her stomach twisting as her nervousness began to grow.

"I can assure you that I have not been ruined, if that is what you mean."

She was not about to tell him the truth, was not about to state that she had *sought* to ruin herself in order to wed a particular gentleman for, given that the *ton* were not truly aware of it, she did not see the need to tell him either.

"That is good." Lord Childers took her hand and, as the dance came to a stop, bowed over it. "You are not ruined, then, you have nothing which society might find questionable about your character and—"

"I am not going to ruin your friend's character or good standing by being associated with him," Prudence interrupted, finding herself more than a little frustrated at these questions. "That is the only reason you wanted to dance with me, then? You wanted to find out why I am standing as a wallflower rather than a young lady out in society?"

Lord Childers grinned at her.

"Yes, precisely. Though I do also enjoy dancing with a beautiful young lady such as yourself."

Prudence blinked, her frustration instantly fading as

she looked into Lord Childers face and at the smile spreading upon it. In a second, she went from feeling a fizzing irritation and an upset over his question to feeling a gentle glowing warmth within her core. It was as though that simple smile, that warmth in his eyes, and the spark there within them had pushed away all of her frustration in a simple second.

A roguish gentleman indeed. Giving herself a slight shake, Prudence sniffed and then nodded in the direction of her mother as the heat within her dissipated.

"Shall we, Lord Childers? Now that you have learned that I am not a ruined young lady?"

"Please, Lady Prudence, I did not mean to insult you."

Prudence looked at him again, seeing a softness about his eyes which made her skin prickle.

"I am sure that you did not. This is a very strange situation, and I can see that you are doing your best to protect your friend." Ignoring the feeling of warmth that swept over her as he took her hand and set it on his arm, Prudence returned her gaze to her mother so that she would not have to even look at Lord Childers. "What is his name, if you please?" Glancing up, she saw him frown, his lip catching between his teeth for just a moment as he hesitated. "Surely there can be no reason for you to hide his name from me now? After all, you have been assured that I am not ruined and–"

"Lord Kingshill," Lord Childers interrupted, rather sharply. "He is Lord Kingshill, and I will introduce you to him just as soon as I am able. Now," he continued, beginning to march across the ballroom, half pulling her along with him, "let me take you to your mother and I shall return soon enough to make the introductions."

"I thank you," Prudence murmured, a little confused as to why Lord Childers was behaving in such a strange manner.

He now appeared to be frustrated by her question about Lord Kingshill, frowning with what might be irritation at her presence. Confused, Prudence chose to remain silent, finding herself relieved when she was once more standing with her mother.

"Good evening, Lady Prudence."

With a nod and without the smile that Prudence had come to expect, Lord Childers turned on his heel and strode away, seemingly determined to escape from her. All the more confused, Prudence frowned and tilted her head, watching him leave – though her mother's heavy sigh broke through her silent thoughts.

"I do not like to see you with that particular gentleman, Prudence."

"I know, Mama," Prudence answered, pulling her gaze away from him. "Though there is good in it, is there not?"

Lady Lymington looked at her sharply.

"Good?"

"Yes," Prudence answered, smiling. "For the *ton* have seen me dancing, have they not? So mayhap, I might be offered more dances."

After a few silent moments of consideration, Lady Lymington began to nod, a smile touching the corners of her mouth.

"I suppose so," she said, with a slight lift of her

eyebrow. "Mayhap the *ton* will wonder what a roguish gentleman is doing dancing with a wallflower." Warming to the idea, her eyes began to sparkle with anticipation. "Mayhap they will ask each other what it is about *you* that has brought such a gentleman to your side! Yes, I can see what you mean, Prudence." With a smile of encouragement, she took Prudence's hand and pressed it lightly. "It may be that this roguish gentleman proves to be the very best thing to happen to you."

CHAPTER SIX

"*Y*ou did not introduce her to me as you had said."

James scowled and waved a hand vaguely.

"It was very busy and I was caught up in another matter."

Lord Kingshill rolled his eyes.

"Might it be that you had *caught* someone up in your arms, forcing me to resign myself to an evening of loneliness?"

Scoffing at this as they walked through Hyde Park, James shook his head.

"I know very well that you would not have been lonely, not in the least."

"Well, I suppose not," Lord Kingshill admitted, though his smile did not return as James had expected. "But that does not mean that I am not disappointed."

"I am sure that you are."

"I do hope," Lord Kingshill continued, turning to look

at James and coming to a stop as they walked, "that you have no intention of keeping the lady from me. Or that you have entirely made up the situation so that I will not fret about my lack of a wife?"

James shook his head.

"I assure you, I have not. I merely became a little distracted yesterday, that was all." He looked back at Lord Kingshill's face, speaking honestly. "I told the lady that I intended to introduce you. I even gave her your title so that she knows who it is that she is to be introduced to!"

Lord Kingshill began to walk again, seemingly placated by what James had told him.

"Very well."

"Good."

James ambled onwards, keeping a smile on his face, and doing his utmost not to linger on the strange tug of his heart which had bothered him a great deal the previous evening. The dance with Lady Prudence had been solely to speak to her privately about why she was a wallflower – an answer she had somewhat reluctantly given – but something about the flash in her green eyes and the touch of pink in her cheeks had given him pause. Disliking that feeling and the awareness that came with it, he had hurried away and had left her standing beside her mother, thinking that the sooner he moved away from the lady, the better it would be.

That had not proven itself to be the case, however. He had walked through the ballroom, looking for some young lady with whom he might dance, tease, and laugh, but his thoughts had been filled with nothing other than Lady Prudence. It had been very odd and, as he had continued to wander around the ballroom, James had found himself somewhat frustrated that he had not been able to remove such thoughts of her from his mind. He had told Lord Kingshill that he had simply been interested in another young lady and had not then been able to find Lady Prudence to bring her to him, but the truth was, he had ignored his responsibility and had set his mind to other things. He had not wanted to be back in company with Lady Prudence, had not wanted to even *glance* at her, in case another look from her green eyes would give him pause and thus, the evening had come to an end without him making the introductions.

"Did she ask anything else about me?"

James looked at his friend, having been lost in his thoughts for some time.

"I beg your pardon?"

"Did she ask anything about me?" Lord Kingshill said again. "This Lady Prudence, did she ask about my title, my social standing, my reputation?"

Chuckling, James shook his head.

"No, she did not. Have no fear, my friend, even if she had done, I would not have told her about your roguish reputation."

A look of relief passed over Lord Kingshill's face.

"Though she is going to find out at some point," James continued, making Lord Kingshill's eyes shadow again. "You will not be able to keep her from that until your wedding day, I can assure you."

"Hmm." Lord Kingshill rubbed his chin with one

hand, his eyes slanting away from James. "That is a consideration."

"Though she is eager to make *any* match," James reminded him. "I am sure that your reputation will not make any difference to her."

Lord Kingshill nodded slowly, then frowned.

"I should be introduced to her just as soon as can be arranged," he said, firmly. "There is no need to delay. I confess that I find myself eager to be free again within society, albeit with a betrothal clinging to me!"

Silently reminding himself that he was doing all of this to make certain that both he and Lord Kingshill could return to their full and free enjoyment of society, James smiled a little tightly.

"Indeed. I assure you that, the moment I see the young lady, I shall make the introduction."

"That would be good. I thank you."

Much to James' relief, Lord Kingshill then began to talk at length about another subject – namely the upcoming evening of cards and gambling at Lord Dickson's townhouse – and left James again to his own thoughts. Listening with only half an ear, he turned his head to the right and then to the left, taking in which other members of society were present, only for his gaze to fall upon the very person they had been speaking about.

Lady Prudence.

"Shall we turn around?"

The words were out of his mouth before he could stop himself, frowning as he said them for, even to his own mind, they made very little sense.

"Turn back already?" Lord Kingshill chuckled and then, much to James' relief – though he did not know where such relief came from – turned about so that he might return along the path they had been walking. "And here I thought you were going to be walking through all of Hyde Park until the fashionable hour, hoping that there would be some young lady good enough to catch your eye!"

James snorted.

"I could have any young lady that I wished in my arms," he said boldly, grinning as his friend spluttered with both indignation and laughter. "Now, let us consider this evening's entertainment – and how we might be able to cheat just a little to gain a good deal more coin than ever before!"

At this, Lord Kingshill laughed aloud, but then immediately began to discuss what it was that he and James might do, and how they might play their particular hand of cards. James settled into the conversation though, much to his irritation, he could not help but glance over his shoulder and take one more look at Lady Prudence.

THERE SHE IS.

"Lady Prudence, good evening." Without having had any sort of intention to walk towards Lady Prudence, James found his feet moving towards her of their own accord. He bowed, waiting for her to bob a curtsey but she did not do anything of the sort. Instead, she simply looked at him, her eyes a trifle narrowed, and her hands clasped tightly in front of her. "I have not yet introduced you to Lord Kingshill, I know," James continued, sighing heavily. "I shall."

"It has been a sennight since we first danced and you found out that I was not ruined," she said, one eyebrow lifting. "And yet you still have not introduced me to Lord Kingshill. I am beginning to wonder if this is something that you have told me for reasons of your own, a situation that is entirely of your own making with, no doubt, a dark and selfish end in mind."

James shook his head, then put one hand on his heart.

"I assure you, I have every intention of introducing you to this gentleman. It is only that I have not yet had the opportunity to do so. Society always demands so much of us, as you know, and–"

"You need not tell me that you and Lord Kingshill are a good deal more popular than I, Lord Childers." She looked away, her shoulders dropping and a heaviness seeming to come into her frame. "I am already well aware of that."

Something like sympathy crept into James' heart though he fought hard to rid himself of it.

"I am glad that you understand." Those words did not seem to have any sort of effect upon Lady Prudence. She did not turn to look at him, did not make any sort of remark but, as James watched, the droop of her shoulders became a little more pronounced, and her head lowered just a fraction more. Guilt tore through him. "I did not mean to injure you." Coming closer to her, James found himself stumbling over his words, seeing the pain that now drew itself across her expression as she finally lifted her eyes to his, only to pull them away again. "It must be rather difficult being a wallflower, I am sure."

Her smile was barely there.

"It can be."

"I – I am sorry for that." He found himself speaking truthfully, his heart feeling a good deal of compassion for what she now expressed. "I have never once thought about what it must be like to be a wallflower."

Slowly, Lady Prudence dragged her gaze to his for the second time, a slight sheen in her eyes.

"It can be rather lonely, I will admit. Though," she continued, blinking quickly and then standing tall, "that does not mean that I should accept all offers of company."

A slight sting whipped across his cheek at her words, but James accepted it, nonetheless. He *was* a scoundrel and could well understand why she would not be agreeable to his company, especially with the warning from her mother.

"I do not mean any harm to you," he said, wondering if she would trust his words even a little. "After all, if I am trying to betrothe you to my friend, do you really think that I would treat you with any sort of disrespect?"

Lady Prudence looked at him for a long moment, only for her lips to quirk at the edges, her eyes burning with a sudden mirth.

"I do not know, Lord Childers. Just how much of a rogue are you?"

This made James laugh, his heart lifting suddenly, filling with a sense of happiness that he had not felt in a long time. Lady Prudence was tenacious, yes, and she was hesitant and uncertain of him, but now, it seemed, there was also a little good humor within her heart.

"I may not have the very best of reputations, Lady Prudence, but I can assure you that I would never betray my friend." He inclined his head just a little, a smile still lingering on his lips. "Therefore, I can promise you that I shall always treat you with respect and consideration."

Lady Prudence's smile grew and, much to James' relief, she nodded.

"Very well, Lord Childers," she said, quietly. "Though you must soon introduce me to this friend of yours so that I know for certain that your words are true."

"I shall do so as soon as I am able," he promised, astonished to find that even though he spoke those words, the reluctance within him grew to such an extent that he could barely stomach the thought of bringing Lady Prudence to Lord Kingshill.

"Might I ask you something else?"

He nodded.

"Of course. I should be glad to answer any questions you have and indeed, would encourage you to ask them of me."

She bit her lip and then looked away.

"I do not mean any insult, but you have said that Lord Kingshill wishes to marry quickly. It also seems that he has not had any opportunity to find a suitable match of his own, which I cannot understand, given his title and standing."

James hesitated, his stomach knotting. He did not dare say too much about Lord Kingshill's reputation, for fear that it would push her away from the idea.

"He is eager to wed because there is a requirement for him to produce an heir," he said, rather bluntly. "A prolonged courtship, followed by betrothal and then, some time thereafter, the marriage, would all take a little too long, to his mind." He shrugged. "Most young ladies of the *ton* wish to be courted. They desire very much to revel in the attentions of whichever gentleman pursues them, and Lord Kingshill has no time for such things." Catching the blossoming heat in the lady's face, James shrugged and looked away. "I am sure that you understand."

"I do, yes."

Her response was so faint that James was not certain he had heard it. What he had just told her had been nothing more than a lie, but it had hidden Lord Kingshill's reputation from her, at least. Trying to douse the quickly igniting guilt within him, James cleared his throat and then gestured to the space beside where she was standing.

"Now, might I join you for a few more minutes? I am sure that, after a few more conversations, you will find me less terrifying and more trustworthy."

She laughed at this, her whole expression altering, light shining in her eyes – and James' breath hitched. It was the first time that he had ever seen her laugh and, as she did so, James almost felt the lingering tension between them fade.

It was both wonderful and disconcerting in equal measure.

"Shall we dance, Lady Prudence?"

Quite where such words had come from, James did

not know, but the desire within him to have her back in his arms was so great that it could not be denied. Lady Prudence's eyes widened, and she looked over his shoulder to where the other guests were already gathering.

"It is the waltz, Lord Childers."

"And you can dance the waltz, can you not?"

She looked at him, blinked, and then frowned.

"Yes, I believe so."

"Then what is to stop us?" He held out his hand to her. "Shall we?"

It took her a moment to respond but, when she did, the smile that spread across her face was so beautiful, it took James' breath away for a moment.

"How very kind of you, Lord Childers," she answered, softly. "I should very much like to dance the waltz with you."

"As should I with you," James murmured, before turning to lead her out to the floor.

CHAPTER SEVEN

"*W*hat a pleasant day it is for a walk, Lady Prudence!"

"Indeed." Prudence glanced at Lord Childers then looked at her mother, who was gazing back at Lord Childers with clear dislike in her expression. They had come upon each other quite by accident and yet, seeing him again so soon after they had danced the waltz together the previous evening made her heart quicken in a most disconcerting way. "It is not yet the fashionable hour and I thought to take a short walk before the *ton* arrives."

"A capital idea! I have always thought that the fashionable hour can get a trifle too busy," Lord Childers answered, though he smiled at Lady Lymington rather than Prudence. "I thought to walk this way. Might you wish – might she be permitted – to join me, Lady Lymington?"

Prudence's heart quickened but she quietened it just as hastily as she could. She was not about to start losing her good sense over one gentleman! That would make very little sense, especially since she was supposedly soon to be wed to his friend.

"Prudence, do you wish to do such a thing?"

The warning in her mother's voice was clear, but Prudence glanced around the park, seeing that there appeared to be very few others present.

"For a short while, Mama," she suggested, as Lady Lymington's lips pressed tightly together. "We are to return home before the fashionable hour anyway, are we not? I will not walk for too long a time."

Lady Lymington sniffed but nodded, leaving Prudence to accept Lord Childers arm and then, to fall into step with him. No doubt her mother was still thinking about what they had discussed between them previously. Lord Childers might well be a means of pushing her back into society and, even though Lady Lymington was clearly disconcerted at the idea of having her daughter walk with a rogue, she did not object.

They walked in silence for a few minutes, though the nearness of him made Prudence's heart squeeze with the memory of being in his arms. They had not spoken a single word to each other all through the waltz, but Lord Childers had never once taken his eyes from hers and she had struggled to look anywhere but up at him. It had been as though the rest of the ballroom had fallen away, that it had only been the two of them upon the floor, and when it had come to an end, there had been so much regret in her heart, it had been like a very sharp, sudden pain piercing right through her.

"A very fine day."

Prudence started, having been lost in her thoughts. "Indeed."

"And with excellent company."

She pressed her lips together, seeing how his gaze was roving around the grounds surrounding them, rather than looking at her. Did he truly feel genuine happiness in being in such pleasant surroundings? Or was he only saying such things in the hope of garnering her interest in him.

"You have not told me why Lord Kingshill wishes to marry so quickly," she said, before their conversation could drift into all manner of things. "You said you would answer any questions I have and, therefore, I should like to ask you why Lord Kingshill has not married as yet. He is a highly titled gentleman and yet he has not found himself a bride. What reason for that is there?"

Finally, Lord Childers looked back at her, surprise lingering in his eyes.

"You mean to ask me about Lord Kingshill's standing?"

Prudence nodded; she felt a tightness in her chest which made it difficult to breathe deeply.

"You asked me about my reasons for being a wallflower," she explained. "I should like to ask why a gentleman with such a high title has not yet considered matrimony. It is clear that this has come to him as a sudden demand, an unexpected desire and I must wonder why he turns to a wallflower rather than to any other young lady of the *ton*. I am looking for the truth as to why such a thing must be."

THE WALLFLOWER'S CHOICE | 71

"I can understand that."

Lord Childers did not give her any further explanation though a frown began to pull at his forehead, making Prudence's heart twist with concern.

"As a wallflower, I confess that I am not entirely aware of all that is going on in society," Prudence continued when he said nothing. "I do hope that you do not think I am prying."

"Of course not." Lord Childers looked at her for a long moment, his eyes steady, but that frown still flickering there. "I confess that I was wondering when this conversation would come about, Lady Prudence. I was hoping that you would not ask, truth be told, but I suppose that I should tell you regardless."

Prudence's heart flipped over in her chest, a sudden tightness – a sudden fear – lurching through her. What was it that he had been hiding from her? What was it that he had wanted to keep hidden? Surely Lord Kingshill did not have some sort of dreadful circumstance clinging to him?

"He is as much a scoundrel as I am, Lady Prudence." With a heavy sigh, Lord Childers looked away. "I am sorry to say it, but that is the truth."

If she had not had her hand on his arm, Prudence was quite sure she would have come to a complete stop. Shock ran through her, her fingers tightening on him as she fought her way through a sudden, blind panic.

I am going to marry a rogue!

"He has hidden a good deal from society, Lady Prudence, but they know him to be something of a rogue, at least," Lord Childers continued, not seeming to understand the pain that suddenly tore through her at his words. "I do not think that you need to fear such a thing, however. After all, you are a wallflower, rejected by society and he is a rogue, also rejected by society."

"They are two entirely different things!"

Prudence could not seem to catch her breath, her heart pounding as cold sweat broke out across her forehead. Lord Childers was saying something to her, but she did not hear him, did not seem to notice his words. Instead, there was nothing but a gentle buzzing in her ears, and she was both hearing and feeling every beat of her heart. Her vision blurred, panic gripping her until, all of a sudden, she could not seem to even take another step.

"Lady Prudence?" Lord Childers released her hand from his arm and turned so he might look down fully into her face, his hands finding both of hers and gripping them tightly. "I have shocked you, I can see. I did not mean to do such a thing. I–"

"I cannot marry a scoundrel!"

Lord Childers held her gaze steadily, saying nothing as she looked back up at him, her breath still coming fast as she battled her overwhelming emotions. Everything that had been built up within her, the faint hope that she might find herself a suitable husband and live a contented, happy life, was all torn away in a single moment.

"What if he is to reform himself?"

The quiet voice of Lord Childers brought her back to the present, looking up at him again as she swallowed tightly.

"I – I do not know."

"A scoundrel still requires a wife. Besides which, the eagerness also comes from the realization that he requires an heir. To find a young lady who will be eager to accept a scoundrel as a husband might be rather difficult and, since he has such an eagerness about this matter, he decided an arrangement would be suitable," he told her, his voice quiet and his expression soft. "And if he will be a rogue no longer, then would that not be a good thing? Yes, it does mean that society will be rather astonished at the match and will, no doubt, whisper about it for a time, but if it is to bring you eternal happiness, then there is no real seriousness to that, is there?" Prudence did not know what to say. The shock still ran through her and, even though his hands were squeezing hers, even though he stood so close to her so that she could feel his breath on her cheek, she could find nothing to say. "Will you still meet him, at the very least?"

Closing her eyes, Prudence nodded slowly.

"I suppose I should still do so, yes."

"I thank you." Lord Childers released her hands and then stepped back. "I can understand your hesitancy, but I can assure you that Lord Kingshill *wants* to marry. I am certain that he understands all that is required of a gentleman who desires such a thing!"

"I must hope so," Prudence murmured, glancing over her shoulder, only to see that her mother was standing with another lady, deep in conversation with her. Little wonder that she had voiced no concern in seeing Prudence and Lord Childers so close together. "I am aware that, as a wallflower, I ought not to care too deeply about who I marry, but all the same, Lord Childers, the thought of being married to a rogue who will care nothing for me and use me only as decoration in front of society's eyes, is not something that I can bear! I believe that, even though I stand to the side, even though the *ton* does not really consider me, I am still worthy of being treated with consideration and respect."

Lord Childers looked at her for a long moment, saying nothing. Then, with a heavy breath, he inclined his head, nodded, and then took her hand again for a brief moment.

"I quite understand, and I agree entirely."

Her eyebrows lifted just a little.

"You do?"

"I do, and I promise you that I shall make that expectation very clear to Lord Kingshill."

A little light relief filled her though, as they stood there, hand in hand, that relief grew into something more. There was a gentle heat that was not unwelcome, curling through her stomach and leaving her sighing with something akin to contentment – though that faded rapidly when Lord Childers took his hand away.

"I must beg to take my leave of you now," he said, softly. "Do excuse me, Lady Prudence. Thank you for walking with me for a time. Mayhap we shall be able to walk together again on another fine day such as this."

"I should like to, yes."

The words came out of her mouth and shocked Prudence utterly. She stared back at Lord Childers as he took his leave and then walked away from her, leaving her staring after him in utter astonishment. What had possessed her to speak in such a way to him? No doubt his suggestion was simply spoken out of propriety, given all that she had said to him before as regards his consideration of her. But now, she had spoken with a fervency as regarded her desire to walk with him again on a fine summer's day, rather than simply remaining silent, as she ought to have done.

Why did I say it? She dropped her head. *Why did I suggest that I would like to be in his company again? I am meant to be considering betrothal to his friend, to Lord Kingshill, rather than enjoying Lord Childers' company! And besides which, he is still nothing but a rogue and I should be doing all that I can to stay far from him.*

Those thoughts, those quiet whispers to herself, did nothing to persuade Prudence's heart to change all it felt, however. Squeezing her eyes closed for a moment, she fought hard to push everything away, to remove every single ounce of feeling... but instead, she was left with nothing but confusion, upset, and to her dismay, a lingering warmth that crept into the very depths of her heart.

PRUDENCE LET out a heavy sigh and shook her head.

"I do not know what to think, Anna."

"I would demand an introduction if I were you!" Miss Rockwell exclaimed as they took tea together in Lord Lymington's drawing room. "It has been almost a fortnight now and all you have done is talk with Lord Childers!"

Yes, I have, Prudence thought to herself, finding a slight smile tilting her lips. *And I have not found that at all disagreeable.*

"Prudence?"

Prudence looked back at her friend, realizing that she had lost herself in her thoughts for a moment.

"Yes?"

"When will you demand a meeting with this gentleman? It seems rather strange to me that he has not met you as yet, especially since there is some haste in his desire to marry."

Considering what she would tell her friend, Prudence took a breath and then spoke.

"It is a little odd, yes, but it has given me a lot of time to think about what my future would be like, should I accept him."

"That, I suppose, is a good thing."

"I do have some concerns," Prudence continued, recalling that she had not yet told Miss Rockwell what she had learned of Lord Kingswell's reputation.

"Oh? It cannot be about his title, I am sure. A Marquess is a very high title indeed."

Prudence shook her head.

"No, it is not."

"Then do you think you cannot believe Lord Childers? That Lord Childers has made up this story for reasons of his own?"

"I confess that I did put that to Lord Childers when I

last spoke to him," Prudence admitted. "He did reassure me, however."

Miss Rockwell scowled, her expression rather dark as she reached to take a sip of her tea before setting it back down again.

"I understand that you have been reassured, but I am not certain that you can trust either Lord Childers or Lord Kingshill. It has taken too long for this introduction. I do not see why Lord Childers cannot simply do as he has said!"

"I think that he will," Prudence answered, a little surprised at how quickly she came to Lord Childers' defense. "He has told me that Lord Kingshill is taking a little time to consider all that has been put to him. Lord Childers explained that it came as something of a surprise, for within only a few days of Lord Kingshill expressing his desire to wed – and to wed quickly – Lord Childers came upon us and then, after he had spoken to me, went to his friend with the news."

"And why is there so much haste?" Miss Rockwell's eyes narrowed just a little. "There *is* a reason for his haste, is there not?"

Prudence nodded.

"He does not desire to court or the like." Something like embarrassment swarmed through her and she reached for her tea to cover it. "He desires to have an heir produced as quickly as possible."

"And yet he takes all this time to consider?" Miss Rockwell clicked her tongue. "I am not certain that such a thing is true."

"There is another reason." Prudence pressed her lips

tightly together, steeling herself for whatever reaction Miss Rockwell would throw at her. "Lord Childers told me that his friend is as much a scoundrel as he is."

Miss Rockwell froze in place, her teacup held halfway between the table and her mouth. She stared back at Prudence with wide eyes and Prudence, feeling her embarrassment rising all the more, simply looked away, unable to bear her friend's astonished look.

"I was terribly shocked," she admitted, when her friend still said nothing. "But Lord Childers has told me that Lord Kingshill will reform himself when he marries. And I, being a wallflower all the same, cannot exactly think of a reason why I ought to refuse him simply because of his reputation." A strangled sound came from her friend, but when Prudence looked at her, waiting for her response, Miss Rockwell simply shook her head. "Not everyone can have the happiness that you have found," Prudence murmured, when Miss Rockwell finally took a sip of her tea. "I will admit to being a little envious of that. While being very glad for you indeed, but my situation is vastly different. I do not have any other gentlemen vying for my hand and nor do I have the prospect of such gentlemen coming to seek me out either! All I have is this rogue pursuing me in the hope that I will agree to marry his friend. And I cannot see a good reason to refuse him."

Miss Rockwell nodded slowly and then, after a moment, let out a slow breath.

"Far be it from me to offer you any advice," she said, softly. "But please, my dear friend, consider all of this with great seriousness and be aware that you are placing a great deal of trust in all that Lord Childers says about Lord Kingshill."

Prudence nodded, a sense of relief washing over her now that she had been honest with her friend.

"Thank you, Anna." She let out another breath, her shoulders dropping just a little. "I swear to you, I shall be."

CHAPTER EIGHT

"*I* think I must meet her. It has been too long now since that idea first came to me."

James lifted an eyebrow.

"I do not think that any such idea came to *you*," he remarked as they walked through the park, reminding James of the conversation he had enjoyed with Lady Prudence not too long ago. "I was the one who suggested it, was I not?"

Lord Kingshill chuckled, though the sound irritated James somewhat.

"Yes, I suppose that is true. I have *you* to thank for this arrangement, though," he continued, shooting James a hard look, "you have not yet introduced me to Lady Prudence. I had even thought that I should, mayhap, wander around the ballroom and speak to each and every wallflower in the hope of meeting her!"

"And you did not?"

His friend snorted.

"Of course I did not! I had other ladies that I was

eager to spend time with and I could not simply set that aside in the hope of meeting Lady Prudence now, could I?" His eyes glittered as he chuckled and though James laughed, something about what his friend had said sank down into his soul and pulled his contentment from him. It was not as though Lord Kingshill had said anything wrong, or was at all insulting in his statement, but rather that James himself was rather unsettled by it. A memory of Lady Prudence came to mind, reminding him of just how shocked and upset she had been to realize that the gentleman she was to wed was nothing other than a rake.

"I did tell her about your reputation."

The smile shattered on Lord Kingshill's face.

"I beg your pardon?"

James shrugged.

"I had no choice. But once I reassured her that you, despite being a rogue, have every desire to be wed and will reform yourself, she appeared a little more contented."

"Reform?" Lord Kingshill scoffed at this at once, shaking his head furiously.

"You know very well that I will not reform myself. The very purpose of my seeking out a bride is simply so that I might then return to my rather enjoyable way of life, doing just as I please while, at the same time, ensuring that my responsibilities as the Marquess of Kingshill are met. That is why I must seek out someone such as Lady Prudence, someone who is willing to marry, but who also *must* marry, so that she can have no complaint about me."

James shook his head, a little concerned over what Lord Kingshill had just said.

"Lady Prudence is afraid that, should she betrothe herself to you, she will find herself wed to a scoundrel."

"Well, to my mind, there is no real concern." Lord Kingshill shrugged and then continued walking. "That is exactly my intention."

"But if you say such a thing to the lady herself, then I can promise you that she will turn her back. You may not even become betrothed!"

"Then I will say nothing which might force such a thing," Lord Kingshill stated, firmly. "Not until we are wed at least."

James said nothing to this response, all too caught up in a great sense of despair – not for his friend, but for Lady Prudence. He did not want her to be in the very sort of marriage that she feared, did not want her to struggle with a husband who cared nothing for her and pursued every other young lady instead.

But I was the one who suggested it.

This new sense of determination, this desire to aid Lady Prudence so that she might gain all that she wanted, flung itself out from James' heart and spread through him. He tried to speak, tried to tell his friend that he now should resolve to improve himself, and that he could no longer continue to pursue nothing more than pleasure and delight, but no words came to him. He could not say anything to Lord Kingshill now, not when he himself had been the one to suggest the idea in the first place! All the same, however, all he could see was the sadness on Lady Prudence's face, the fear lingering in her eyes. What was he to do? And why did he feel so strongly about it all?

"You are not listening to me."

James looked at Lord Kingshill.

"Forgive me. I was too caught up in my own thoughts."

"No doubt about the ladies *you* are pursuing at present," Lord Kingshill chuckled, as he looked at James. "Is there anyone in particular?"

James said nothing for a moment, smiling and nodding as two young ladies, walking arm in arm, passed them.

"I shall not reveal them to you," he said, after a moment, "for fear that you will–"

"Did you hear them speak?"

James frowned.

"The two young ladies?"

Lord Kingshill nodded, a sudden spark of excitement coming into his eyes.

"I could have sworn that one of them said, 'Lady Prudence'." He stopped suddenly, putting one hand out to stop James from continuing to walk. "Pray, tell me if she is nearby. Look! Many others are beginning to gather in the park. Is she present?"

A roar of uncertainty filled James' heart, and he quickly shook his head.

"No, I do not think so."

"Are you sure? You did not even look!"

A little unsure of why he was suddenly so reluctant to permit his friend to meet Lady Prudence, James swallowed hard, lifted his gaze, and looked about the park.

His heart slammed into his chest as his eyes suddenly caught hers and he snatched in a breath, garnering a look of surprise from his friend.

"She is here, then?"

Trying to throw away his sudden, strong emotions, James gestured to Lady Prudence with a lift of his chin.

"It seems as though you will have your desire answered this very afternoon!"

It is not as though I could never introduce them, he told himself, as Lord Kingshill rubbed his hands together in evident anticipation. *That would be foolishness.*

"Oh?" Lord Kingshill looked first to James and then out to where he was gazing. "You mean to say that *she* is Lady Prudence? The one standing with only another young lady beside her?"

"Yes, that is she. With the brown hair."

"My word."

With a frown, hearing the shock in Lord Kingshill's voice, James looked at his friend sharply.

"You do not mean to suggest that there is something wrong with her countenance, do you?"

"No, of course not! I confess that I did not expect her to be so fair!"

James said nothing, walking forward alongside his friend, finding that he was frowning without any real understanding as to why. With a clearing of his throat, he made certain that his countenance was calm, just as Lady Prudence glanced towards them – and then looked at them for a second time, her eyes widening just a little.

"Good afternoon, Lady Prudence." James inclined his head, looking then at Miss Rockwell who seemed to be ever present with Lady Prudence herself. "And to you also, Miss Rockwell."

"Good afternoon."

Bobbing a curtsey, Lady Prudence exchanged a glance with her friend and then turned to look at James, her gaze drifting towards Lord Kingshill. James, turning slightly, gestured to his friend, battling against the restraint within him. It was as if he quietly wanted to keep them separated from each other, though he had no real reason as to why that might be.

Foolishness, James reminded himself before, forcing a smile, he gave the introductions. Watching Lady Prudence as she looked again to Lord Kingshill, taking him in with those soft, green eyes of hers, James felt his eyebrows drop low over his brows again.

"Good afternoon, Miss Rockwell, Lady Prudence." Lord Kingshill bowed low. "It is a great honor to meet you."

"As it is to be introduced to you," came the quiet reply, though Miss Rockwell, James noticed, was frowning heavily. "Thank you, Lord Childers, for doing so."

James said nothing, giving her only a small nod as he then pulled his gaze away. There was much to be said between Lord Kingshill and Lady Prudence and he did not need to stand here and be a part of it. He had done as he had been asked. He had introduced Lord Kingshill to Lady Prudence and now, he need not spend even a moment longer in her company. Without so much as a word to either Lord Kingshill or to the two young ladies, James turned and began to walk away, his frown returning for what was the third time in only a few minutes.

I am free now, he told himself, firmly. *Free to do as I please, knowing that soon, Lord Kingshill will be able to join me.* Letting his gaze rove around the park, he took a deep breath and set his shoulders. *Now all I need to do is find something... or someone to entertain me.*

CHAPTER NINE

*W*atching as Lord Childers walked away, Prudence looked back at Lord Kingshill's face, seeing the broad grin that spread across it and finding herself inwardly recoiling.

Lord Kingshill did not have a kind expression, nor was there any softness about his eyes. Instead, there was a hardness there, a glitter in the depths of his dark brown eyes which Prudence did not like in the least.

"Excellent, excellent indeed!" His eyes roved over her, and Prudence shivered lightly, appreciating Miss Rockwell's presence and support. "Now, Lady Prudence, since we have met, it may well be time for us to discuss what it is to take place between us!"

Prudence swallowed once, twice, and then a third time in an attempt to remove the ache from her throat.

"Indeed." Her chin lifted just a little as she fought to find more strength. "I hear that you are something of a rake, Lord Kingshill. I am sure that you are aware that such a reputation carries a great many shadows with it?

Shadows which will cling to me, the moment that we announce our connection." To her very great surprise, Lord Kingshill only shrugged. Miss Rockwell caught her breath in obvious astonishment and then looked to Prudence who, in return, could only give her a small shake of her head. "You do know that your roguish reputation must begin to fade away, I am sure," Prudence continued when Lord Kingshill said nothing. "I have been assured by Lord Childers that—"

"You need not be concerned, Lady Prudence. I will do what I must to reform myself, I promise you." Waving one hand as if to dismiss her, Lord Kingshill took a small step closer. "So, we are to become betrothed, yes?"

Prudence blinked.

"I – I suppose that—"

"I think it would be best to have a courtship, albeit a very short one." Miss Rockwell glanced at Prudence, her eyes flashing a warning. "You do not want the *ton* to wonder why there is so sudden a betrothal between you. That might add all the more to the rumors which already pursue you, Lord Kingshill."

The gentleman frowned.

"Such rumors do not weigh heavily on me, I confess. I do not think that there is any need to delay."

"Ah, but they might cling to your heir," Miss Rockwell responded, quickly. "And I am certain that you do not want that to occur."

Lord Kingshill hesitated, then rubbed one hand over his chin, his eyes slanting back towards Miss Rockwell as though he did not much like what she had said.

"I suppose that is a consideration."

"Good. Then a courtship?" Miss Rockwell looked first to Prudence and then to Lord Kingshill again, her eyebrows lifted. "For a short while, of course."

"Very well." Lord Kingshill sighed and then looked at Prudence. "I presume that you will tell your parents about our intentions?"

Prudence's hands curled into fists as she fought to control her surprise.

"I – I had thought that you would wish to speak to my father yourself."

Lord Kingshill shook his head.

"No, no. There is too much to explain and I shall leave that to you to do. If your father refuses to give his permission, however, then we will be at an end anyway and that would mean a waste of my time and my efforts. No, Lady Prudence, I think it would be best if you spoke to your parents about this matter." Clearing his throat, he turned his head away and then, evidently spying someone, gave them a wave of his hand and, after a moment, glanced back at Prudence and Miss Rockwell. "I shall take my leave of you now. Good afternoon."

"Good afternoon," Prudence echoed, finding her heart aching as she watched Lord Kingshill walk away.

He was not at all as she had expected, for even a rogue could be charming and well-mannered! Was not Lord Childers all of those things? Lord Kingshill, on the other hand, was nothing more than a rude, inconsiderate fellow who appeared to be a little lazy. Why was he asking *her* to speak to her parents about their potential betrothal? It ought to fall on his shoulders rather than on Prudence's. What would her father think of her speaking to him in such a way? It made very little sense.

"Well?"

Prudence looked at her friend, seeing the doubt flickering in her eyes.

"I thought him rather rude," she admitted, tears beginning to burn. "I do not know what I expected, but I certainly did not expect this!"

"He was inconsiderate, thoughtless, and dismissive," Miss Rockwell stated, perhaps unaware of the pain that her words sparked in Prudence. "I am surprised that he was so unwilling to speak with your father and instead, asked you to do such a thing as that! It seems very strange to me that a gentleman would be so improper in what is an important matter!"

"I shall have to speak to my parents," Prudence murmured, reaching to pinch the bridge of her nose. "I do not know what they will say. My mother already warned me away from Lord Childers; I expect that she will say the same about Lord Kingshill."

"Though Lord Childers was not offering matrimony," Miss Rockwell added, her expression still heavy. "It may be different for Lord Kingshill."

"Yes, it may be," Prudence agreed, slowly uncurling her fingers, and stretching out her hands again. "I suppose all we can do is wait and see."

～

"I MUST SPEAK TO YOU, MAMA."

Lady Lymington glanced over her shoulder as the maid set a pearl necklace around her neck.

"Good evening, Prudence. You are prepared, yes? We are to leave for Lord Venables' ball very soon and I do not want to keep your father waiting."

Prudence came a little further into the room, glancing at the maid and waiting for her mother to dismiss her. Lady Lymington said nothing, watching Prudence carefully and, when she rose, turned to glance at herself in the mirror before sending the maid away.

"What is the matter, Prudence?" she asked, coming to take one of Prudence's hands in her own, her eyes steady. "I understand that there is difficulty for you in this, but it must be done. We must continue to attend social occasions in the hope that society will begin to welcome you back again."

"It is not about society, Mama," Prudence answered, a knot tying itself in her stomach. "It is something a little more... personal."

Lady Lymington frowned.

"Has something happened to you?"

"Not in any dreadful manner, no," Prudence reassured her. "I have had a gentleman speaking with me. He wishes to move forward to courtship."

In an instant, everything about her mother's expression changed. Her eyes went wide, a huge smile spread across her face, and she squeezed Prudence's hand tightly.

"Really? A gentleman?"

Prudence nodded.

"Yes, Mama. Though there is a reason for his urgency

so please do not think that this is as wonderful as it seems."

At once, Lady Lymington's face went white, her expression crumpling.

"Pray tell me that he has not sought to take advantage of you!"

"No, no, nothing like that. I am quite safe." Offering her mother a reassuring smile, Prudence pushed down her nervousness and continued to explain. "He is attempting to reform himself but, given that no young lady will wed him due to his reputation, he seeks out an immediate match."

"A rake?" Lady Lymington's voice was hoarse now, her fingers gripping Prudence's so tightly, it was a little painful. "You are being pursued by a rake?" Her eyes widened all the more. "Tell me it is not Lord Childers!"

"It is not. It is Lord Kingshill."

Her mother closed her eyes tightly and dragged in a shaking breath. "Oh, my dear!"

"But he is going to reform himself, Mama," Prudence protested, aware of the reluctance within her own heart. "At least, that is what he has said."

"And you believe him?" Lady Lymington released Prudence's hands, only to throw her own hands up in frustration. "How could you be so foolish? You cannot for a *moment* believe that there is any truth in that!"

Prudence swallowed hard, heat building behind her eyes.

"I have no other choices, Mama."

This gave Lady Lymington pause. Her hands fell to her sides, and she grew very still.

"Lord Childers was the one who brought us together," Prudence continued, quietly, "though I was not introduced to Lord Kingshill until recently. He wishes me to talk to my father about the arrangement. For the moment, we should like to court and–"

"There is nothing wrong with being a spinster." Lady Lymington hurried forward again, catching Prudence's hands. "I know it will be difficult but–"

"Both you and father believe it would be best for me to marry," Prudence interrupted, albeit speaking as gently as she could. "This gentleman, though he is a rogue, is to reform himself. He wishes to have an heir and therefore, though I confess to being uncertain about it all, I can see the benefits of such a marriage."

"But you cannot trust a rake's word," her mother said, fervently, her eyes searching Prudence's. "There is no promise that he will do as he says, no promise that he truly *will* return to gentlemanly ways."

Prudence nodded.

"I understand that, Mama, and I appreciate it a great deal – more than you can know. I do not look forward to marrying Lord Kingshill, for I do not think that he is a particularly kind or considerate gentleman, but I would still be wed, would I not? I would still have my own home and the chance of having children."

"I can see the pull of that, but your husband would be a scoundrel! That would bring you a great deal of pain. I should prefer to see evidence of it, such as I have seen in Lord Childers of late, before I permitted you to make any genuine, long-lasting commitment. I am sure that your father will feel the same."

A little surprised, Prudence looked back at her mother.

"You have seen something in Lord Childers?"

"I have," Lady Lymington answered, though she spoke slowly as though she was uncertain of why Prudence was asking such a thing. "Only of late, however. He has been taking a good deal of interest in you, has he not? He has been speaking with you, laughing with you, and has even danced with you on occasion. I have been concerned about his company as you know, but what I have seen of him, and even what society has been speaking of, seems to suggest that he has stepped back from that roguish way of living for a time – though I am not convinced by it."

A gentle heat began to rise in Prudence's chest, and she found her lips curving, though she tried her best to hide it from her mother. Why was it that hearing such things about Lord Childers made her heart sing in such a ridiculous way? Why was it that she found herself delighting in this news, thrilled to hear that her mother thought a little more highly of Lord Childers than she had done before? He was not the one she was to court, so why should she have any sort of interest in him?

"I will have to speak to your father about this, but I can assure you that he will not be in the least bit pleased," Lady Lymington stated, firmly. "However, whether or not he will agree, I cannot say." She shook her head and sighed. "How much I wish that this situation was different for you, my dear. If only you could be back in society just as you ought to be!"

A little surprised at the sympathy with which her mother spoke, Prudence shook her head.

"Mama, I deserve this. I was foolish, I was selfish, and I was unkind. I am glad that society does not know the true extent of my folly, but all the same, I am well aware that the consequences that I have brought upon myself are perfectly fair."

Her mother pressed her lips together for a few moments.

"I have been very harsh with you in this matter, have I not?" she said, her voice holding more gentleness within it than Prudence had heard in a long time. "I am sorry for that. I will do all that I can to support you, my dear, and if this is what you wish and if it is what you truly desire, I will not refuse you. Only do be careful, I beg of you. I would not want to see you brokenhearted and sorrowful."

Struggling against sudden tears, Prudence embraced her mother tightly, sensing a healing growing between them.

"Thank you, Mama," she murmured, softly. "I promise you, I will take the greatest care."

CHAPTER TEN

"I swear, Childers, if you do not remove this heaviness from yourself, then I simply will not attend with you this evening. You can take your own carriage."

James scowled and then picked up his glass of brandy.

"I am quite contented. I do not know what it is that you are speaking of."

"I am sure that you do." Lord Kingshill threw back his brandy and then set the glass down on the table by his side. "Ever since I arrived, you have been in some dark mood and, quite frankly, I have no interest in being in your company if you are going to continue in this way."

Refilling his brandy glass, James lifted it in a half toast.

"I can assure you, my friend, that this brandy will help my mood a great deal."

He took a sip and watched as his friend frowned at him, but much to James' surprise, he found that he did not care. Ever since Lord Kingshill had stepped into the room, James had found his mind filled with a heaviness that he could not explain. It had only worsened as Lord Kingshill had spoken of what he had shared with Lady Prudence, to the point that James now found himself not in the least bit inclined towards his friend's company. Not that he could tell him such a thing, however, for to speak of his present feelings when he was so utterly confused would not be wise.

"So, are you going to tell me of your reasons for your present disinclination or are you going to leave me to guess?"

James rolled his eyes.

"As I have said, I am quite well."

"But you are not acting as though you are," his friend said, a little more quietly. "If something is troubling you, then why do you not speak to me of it? We are friends, are we not?"

Looking sidelong at his friend, James sat down and then shrugged.

"I do not…" Trailing off, he shook his head to himself and then sighed. Was it worth telling Lord Kingshill the truth, albeit without mentioning Lady Prudence's name? Perhaps Lord Kingshill would be able to offer some advice. After all, the only thing James wanted was to remove Lady Prudence from his thoughts. "I will confess that there is a desire growing within my heart for one particular lady. And I do not like it."

Lord Kingshill's eyebrows rose high.

"Goodness."

"It is very strange and a good deal irritating," James

continued, his face flushing hot as he tried to find a way to explain himself without giving too much detail away. "This young lady has caught my attention, though there is nothing remarkable about her. I do not *want* to be thinking about her and I certainly have no intention of pursuing her! That is not the sort of gentleman I am and not the sort of gentleman I want to be either!"

Much to his surprise, Lord Kingshill chuckled, making him scowl all the more.

"Goodness, I did not think that I would ever hear such words from your lips! How can it be that you have an affection for a young lady?! Do you know what it is you are giving up?"

"I am not giving up anything, aside from these feelings!" James exclaimed, anger beginning to burn hot within him. "I have no *affection,* as you call it. There is nothing within me like that, I can assure you!"

His friend shrugged.

"Whatever you wish to call it, it is clear that you have some feelings for this young lady, whoever she is." He smiled broadly, his eyes twinkling with evident mirth, which only made James' anger bubble with fury. "Might I ask who this lady is?"

James folded his arms over his chest.

"I was looking for your advice as to how I might rid myself of this but instead, all you do is seek to mock me."

"I do not mock you, I assure you!" Lord Kingshill continued to grin, though he settled back in his chair now, rather than showing any eagerness to depart. "You wish for my advice then? You want to know how to rid yourself of such feelings?"

"I do." James let his hands drop back to his lap. "As I have said, I have no desire for these emotions. I told you of them because you are my friend, not because I wish to be teased about them."

"Very well." Lord Kingshill rubbed his hands together, his smile finally beginning to fade. "Might I suggest that you go and garner the attention of someone else entirely?"

James blinked, his eyebrows lifting.

"You mean I should go and spend some time with another young lady this evening?"

His friend shrugged.

"Why not? I am sure that, should you do so, then you will soon begin to forget about all that you feel." He tilted his head and then began to smile. "It may be more that your attention must be focused on *more* than one young lady, but I am certain that you shall soon find yourself back to as you always have been."

"That is, in fact, a good thought," James admitted, speaking a little more quietly as he considered the upcoming evening. "I think you may be right, Kingshill."

"Good!" Lord Kingshill rose to his feet. "Then are we to attend this soiree?"

"Yes," James stated, firmly. "Let us go. I am sure I will be able to find an interesting young lady to speak to very quickly indeed!"

"A WONDERFUL EVENING, YES," James murmured, moving a little closer to Lady Juliette as he smiled down into her eyes. "You have been wonderful company, Lady Juliette."

"I am glad to hear it."

Lady Juliette smiled back at him only to then move away a little, putting the correct distance between them.

James' heart began to sink towards the ground, his shoulders dropping just a little. Clearly, Lady Juliette had no intention of letting him get close to her, even though she *had* done such a thing before. In fact, James had stolen the smallest of kisses from her once, some months ago and now, this evening, had thought he might try to do so again, given Lord Kingshill's advice. Anything to remove the thought of Lady Prudence from his thoughts.

"Should you like to walk with me for a few minutes?" he asked, leaning down towards her, his arm put out towards her. "I should be very glad of your company."

Lady Juliette looked up at him, her eyes gleaming gently.

"You are very generous, Lord Childers. Might I ask if you have any genuine interest in me, however?"

A little confused at the question, James frowned.

"Of course I do."

"But you do not think of courtship or the like?"

Surprised, James hesitated and then shook his head.

"I confess that I do not think of any such thing as that, not yet, at least."

Lady Juliette took another step away from him, her arms folded.

"So you will do all that you can to capture me in your

arms but you have no thought of pursuing me in a genuine, proper manner?"

All the more confused, James took a few moments to answer, looking at her and wondering why she was asking him such things when, previously, she had been very willing indeed to let him pull her close to him.

"You are aware that I am looking for a husband, I suppose?" Lady Juliette lifted one eyebrow, her lips pursing as James frowned heavily. "I thought that, in permitting you such liberties, I might find myself favored by you. After all, you are a Marquess, and to have a Marquess as my husband would be rather delightful, I am sure. But you, however, encouraged an intimacy with me and thereafter, I found myself entirely forgotten! I was certain I saw you laughing and teasing the widowed Lady Huntington only the day after our... moment... and now, for whatever reason, you have come back to me, no doubt hoping that I would permit you the same liberties again. Yes?"

Greatly astonished at the young lady's fervor, and her bold manner, James found himself quite at a loss as to what to say. He tried twice to speak, tried twice to offer her an explanation but instead, all that came from him was a gruff exclamation which made very little sense whatsoever.

"I see."

Lady Juliette blinked rapidly, making heat rush into James' face as he realized the significance of what he had done. Lady Juliette had thought more would come from his interest in her, and yet, when it had not and she had found herself rejected, that had injured her severely.

James frowned, looking away from Lady Juliette's white face. He had never cared about such things before. Why should he do so now? It was not as though she was the first young lady he had taken liberties with! No doubt there were more than a few young ladies who had all been expecting a little more from him, but he had never once given their view of him any sort of consideration, and there was certainly no desire nor intention for him to do that now. Steeling himself, James inclined his head just a little.

"My dear Lady Juliette, I did not think that you were seeking anything more than a brief connection," he said, seeing how she kept her gaze turned away from him. "I was certain that you understood–"

"Do not for a *moment* think that you shall place the blame for this present situation upon my shoulders!" Lady Juliette hissed, stepping closer to him now, her eyes like shards of broken glass. "You did not truly believe that it was *I* who sought only a brief connection! That was what *you* wanted and yet your sweet words and kindness to me made me believe that courtship was in your thoughts. It was a deliberate deception, and I am not about to take any sort of responsibility for it. Now, kindly take your leave of me and do not think to come near me again."

Her face white, she held his gaze steadily, anger pouring from her towards him, and James, still somewhat astonished, lifted both his hands in defense.

"I shall never speak a word to you again, Lady Juliette, I swear," he mumbled, suddenly at a bit of a loss as regarded what he ought to do next. Such a thing had never happened to him before! Never once had he had any young lady speaking to him in such a way, never had he felt such anger and vehemence being directed towards him. He was known to be a rogue, known to be a scoundrel of the highest order. What had made Lady Juliette believe that she was going to capture his heart?

With a sigh, James turned around, only to come face to face with Lady Prudence. She, being a wallflower, had been standing at the side of the room and James had not noticed her there when he had suggested to Lady Juliette that they come to stand together in the shadows.

For some reason, a great swell of embarrassment rose up within him, filling his heart and making it squeeze painfully. He did not seem to know where to look and struggled to keep his gaze on her, given the expression which was spreading across her face. It was not as though she despised him, not as if she were berating him, only that she seemed almost sad, perhaps disappointed, to see the sort of gentleman that he was. James tried to brush off that particular feeling, tried to tell himself that he owed her nothing, but all the same, the feeling would not leave him. Swallowing hard, he turned away from her also, and strode across the room, suddenly desperate to leave the soiree – and everyone in it – far behind him.

CHAPTER ELEVEN

*P*rudence sat quietly on the bench and looked out across the grounds. Lord Kingshill sat beside her, but though they had sat together for some minutes – and with her mother a short distance away – not a single word had been spoken between them.

"I – I know that this is all a little unusual," Prudence said, her stomach twisting as Lord Kingshill let out a long sigh. "We have not yet begun a proper courtship but–"

"You did speak to your father, did you not?" Lord Kingshill looked at her sharply, his eyes a little narrowed. "I do hope there is to be no difficulty there."

Prudence blinked, her fingers twisting together as she looked at Lord Kingshill, seeing how his jaw had tightened.

"There is no difficulty there, no, I assure you. My father is not particularly pleased, given your reputation, but the courtship can begin whenever you wish it."

She had spoken with her father and mother the

previous evening, only a short time after she had witnessed Lord Childers attempting to pull a young lady into his arms. The pain that had shot through her upon witnessing such a thing had been so great that she had not been able to breathe for some moments. He had twisted about and walked away without a word, and she had also hurried across the room and as far from Lord Childers as she could, all the while berating herself for her foolish emotions.

Her decision had been made for her, she realized. Any sort of feelings she had for Lord Childers were worth nothing, for he did not care for her in the least. Charming and considerate he had appeared to be, but Prudence had let herself be captured by him, albeit just a little. Thus, in her embarrassment and shame, she had spoken to her parents and made it plain that yes, she did want to accept Lord Kingshill's offer of courtship. There had been much discussion but, in the end, Prudence had been given permission by her father to do as she had asked. He had expressed his discontent that Lord Kingshill had not come to speak to him personally, and Prudence had acknowledged that it had not been done properly.

That was all she had been able to say.

"I will tell the *ton* that we are courting this evening, I think." Lord Kingshill sniffed and then threw a glance at her. "There is no requirement for us to be seen together, however, not at balls and soirees or any other evening activity. I will call on you at times, however, to take tea and the like. And mayhap we should go out in the carriage so we can be seen, or a walk in the park as we have done today. But aside from that, I do not see any reason for us to be often in company."

Prudence's mouth went dry, and her heart began to pound. The gentleman had not asked her what she thought about such a thing but had, instead, simply told her that this was what was required and what she was expected to agree to.

"You do not want to spend time with me?" she asked, her voice a little hoarse. "I thought that, since we are looking to betrothal and marriage, you might be eager to do so."

Lord Kingshill chuckled, though the sound was not a pleasant one, making Prudence wince.

"My dear Lady Prudence, I do not think that there is any real reason for us to be very well acquainted, do you?"

"We... we are to be husband and wife," Prudence stammered, rather stunned by his response. "Do you not think that a good reason?"

With a shrug, Lord Kingshill let out a huff of breath.

"I do not think that is reason enough, no. From my point of view, a husband and his wife need not often be in company together and, besides which, you will soon have a son or daughter to care for." He looked at her properly then, a small smile on his face as though this was just what she ought to have expected from him. "I am sure that you are looking forward to being mistress of Kingshill Manor? You will have the entire house to manage, as well as your own quarters."

"My own quarters," Prudence repeated, a little breathlessly.

This, she realized, was Lord Kingshill's hope and expectation: that she would live with him but not be at all present beside him. Instead, they would live two very separate lives while sharing the same house and gardens. It was not at all the sort of life she expected and, were she to be honest with him, she would say that she was both disappointed and horrified to hear it.

"Well, I think I shall take my leave. Good afternoon, Lady Prudence."

Prudence's mouth fell open, her shock so great that she could not even find the words to respond. She stared at the retreating figure of Lord Kingshill, finding her heart aching terribly. The gentleman had not even the smallest consideration for her! He had not asked her if she had anything to speak of, had not asked her for her opinion on anything that he had said, and had made it quite clear that he had no interest in her company – and would not have any interest in the future either! Was that the life that she wanted? Was that the future she was destined for? To marry a gentleman who would not even *look* at her? Whose only interactions with her would be to visit her bedchamber in the hope of producing an heir?

"Goodness, did something happen?"

Prudence looked up as her mother approached, a little embarrassed at how swiftly Lord Kingshill had taken his leave.

"No, Mama."

"Then why did Lord Kingshill walk away so quickly?"

Not certain what to say – for she did not want to tell

her mother the truth, given the shame that would then soon burn through her, Prudence offered a small smile.

"He had some business matters to attend to which were very urgent. This evening, he intends to announce to the *ton* that we have begun a courtship."

"I see." Lady Lymington did not appear to believe this excuse, given the way her eyebrows dropped and her lips flattened. "And what say you, my dear? Are you going to be content with that? Are you going to be glad when he begins to tell the gentlemen and ladies of the *ton* that you are now courting?"

Prudence tried to say yes, tried to tell her mother that this was what she wanted, but the ache in her throat grew and knotted until all she could do was force a smile. It was not one that her mother believed, however, for she sat down and immediately put one arm around Prudence's shoulders.

"My dear girl, you do not have to do this."

Closing her eyes, Prudence fought tears.

"I must," she whispered, unable to trust her voice. "I have no other choice."

"We may yet find someone else. We may find—"

"No, we will not." Prudence shook her head, dropping it forward. "Mama, if I want a family, even with a less than pleasing husband, then this is the only way. You know that there are no other gentlemen eager to pursue me. You can tell that there is no hope of me securing another match." The memory of seeing Lord Childers pursuing the young lady, showing himself to be the rogue that he had proclaimed himself to be, struck her hard and a fresh rush of upset filled her. Upset at herself, for having allowed any sort of feeling to build for Lord Childers and frustration at her foolishness. A tear fell to her cheek but, drawing in a deep breath, Prudence set her shoulders, refusing to let another one fall. "I will accept Lord Kingshill's courtship, knowing that the future will, I pray, bring me a home and children. That is a blessing that I will not gain any other way." She tried not to think about how such a thing would come about and all that she would have to endure, her chin wobbling as she forced a smile. "I am determined."

"GOOD EVENING."

Prudence turned, starting in surprise as Lord Childers bowed to her.

"Lord Childers." She put one hand to her heart instinctively, feeling it jumping wildly within her. "I – good evening."

She curtsied quickly, trying not to look into his face as she rose. Not knowing what else to say, Prudence kept her gaze on his shoulder, wondering what it was that he wished to say to her.

"Lady Prudence." Lord Childers hesitated, then cleared his throat gruffly. "Lady Prudence, I know that there was a little awkwardness before but–"

"Let us not speak of such things," Prudence interrupted quickly, still keeping her gaze on his shoulder. "There is no need to explain yourself. I am well aware of your reputation."

Lord Childers coughed this time, rubbing one hand

over his hair.

"I – I am not certain that... well, if you do not wish to speak of it, then I shall respect that. Though I should like to beg your forgiveness for any embarrassment."

"There was none." Turning her head away, Prudence let herself look out at the ballroom, her hands clasping together in front of her, her fingers twisting just a little. "Pray excuse me, Lord Childers. This evening is rather significant, and I want to be prepared when Lord Kingshill comes to find me."

She felt rather than saw him step closer, his nearness to her sending a slight tremor up her spine. Berating herself for the feelings which then rushed back towards her heart, she steeled herself inwardly, trying to bring to mind what she had seen of him in pursuit of another young lady.

"You expect Lord Kingshill to announce your courtship this evening?"

Nodding, Prudence kept silent.

"Might I ask if you are a little anxious about it?"

She glanced at him, rather surprised at the question.

"A little."

She did not feel the need to tell him anymore, letting his gaze catch hers for just a moment before she looked away again.

"I hope that you will be happy." Without meaning to, without having had any intention of giving any reaction, Prudence found herself snorting in a most unladylike fashion before then covering her face with her hands, her shoulders rounding as heat poured into her face. After a moment or two of silence, she dropped her hands again but said nothing, refusing to look at him. Silently, she begged him to leave, but it seemed that Lord Childers did not hear her quiet hopes, instead moving a little closer so that they stood arm to arm. "I am sorry if there is something which has happened to upset you." He hesitated, then moved again so that he was looking at her a little more closely, his eyes searching her face, though Prudence could not seem to bring her gaze to his. "Lord Kingshill told me... well, that is to say that I thought he might be eager to reform himself after a particular conversation we had. Have you received something different from him?"

"I do not think that Lord Kingshill cares about what I think," Prudence found herself saying, uncertain as to why she was telling him this, but continuing regardless. "He has already decided what sort of marriage we shall have, and it is one where we are entirely separate." She shuddered, her eyes closing for a moment. "For the most part, at least." Lord Childers blew out a breath that brushed warmth across Prudence's cheek and when she opened her eyes to look at him, she saw nothing but a dark scowl across his face, as though he was truly frustrated by what she had told him. "This does not concern you, however," she continued, a little dully. "There is no need for you to consider anything I have said. You have made the arrangement for your friend and–"

"I do not want you to be unhappy."

Prudence gazed back at him, no longer struggling to look into his face.

"I do not believe that you have any requirement to be concerned for me, Lord Childers. Do you not have enough here in society to satisfy you? Do you not have enough to keep your mind... and your heart... occupied?"

He flushed then, clearly well aware of what it was that she spoke of.

"That does not mean that I cannot be concerned for you also, Lady Prudence. In fact, I swear to you now that I shall dedicate myself to making certain that all shall go well for you and that your happiness is made complete."

Prudence, a little surprised, kept her gaze steady as she looked at him.

"I do not know what you mean by that."

"I mean it as simply as it sounds," he replied, taking another step closer to her. "This was my suggestion, this was my doing as regards Lord Kingshill, and the arrangement between you. If my friend has now decided that he will not act in the manner that he ought to, then I will make it my sole purpose to ensure that things change in that regard. I will not look to my own entertainments, I will not focus on my own thoughts and determinations. Instead, I will be at Lord Kingshill's side, guiding and berating him if I must!"

A slight flicker of hope grew in Prudence's heart.

"You would berate your friend?"

"I would." Lord Childers offered her the smallest of smiles, though his gaze remained steady. "This was my doing, Lady Prudence, and I am determined that you should not suffer because of it. As I have said, I will give up all of my considerations and entertainments. You may find this difficult to believe, which I well understand given the fact that I am a gentleman with a dreadful reputation, but this is the only thing that I desire to do."

THE WALLFLOWER'S CHOICE | 113

Not quite certain what to say, Prudence took a moment, her mouth going dry at the intensity of his gaze. All that she had felt before began to return to her heart with a swiftness that told her she had never really been free of it. She wanted to cry out in frustration, wanted to exclaim aloud that she was nothing but a fool but instead, she simply nodded.

"I would very much like to believe you, Lord Childers."

"I shall prove myself to you, Lady Prudence." Without warning, Lord Childers reached out and took her hand, bending over it before she had time to react. His breath ran hot on her skin, her whole body suddenly tingling with a strange awareness and a growing desire which she instantly tried to douse. "From this moment on, I am devoted to you."

Was it just her own mind, or did he take a little too long to release her hand? Prudence licked her lips, looking away as she fought to find words, her heart quickening in her chest, her skin burning.

"I – I thank you, Lord Childers."

"And now I shall take my leave of you, and go in search of Lord Kingshill," Lord Childers continued, looking away from her. "I must make certain that this announcement, if it is to be made, will be done properly. Do excuse me."

With a flash of a smile in her direction, Lord Childers hurried away at once, clearly determined to do just as he had said. Prudence watched after him, her heart already betraying her all over again.

CHAPTER TWELVE

"What is this?"

"I must speak with you. Now."

James found himself frowning as he grabbed his friend's arm and tugged him away from the four ladies he had been speaking with. It was not that there was any sort of surprise in seeing his friend behave so, only that he found himself to be a little frustrated even though there was no legitimate reason for him to be so.

"Whatever is the matter?"

Lord Kingshill waved one hand vaguely, his eyes a little hooded and, inwardly, James felt himself groan.

"You are not in your cups, are you?"

Lord Kingshill scowled.

"What does it matter if I am?"

"I thought you were to make an announcement this evening. I thought you were to tell the *ton* about your betrothal."

"And I am."

"In this state?"

His friend narrowed his eyes, his jaw tightening.

"Why does my behavior matter to you?"

It was not a question that James could answer. It was not one that he *wanted* to answer, but all the same, it was required of him.

"I care... I care about your standing in society as a soon-to-be married man," he said, a little lamely. "You do not want to embarrass yourself, or the lady in question, now, do you?"

It was not a particularly good excuse but, after a moment, his friend appeared to accept it. This might well have been from his own slightly inebriated state but, all the same, James was relieved.

"I suppose I can understand that." Lord Kingshill sighed and shook his head. "Very well, I shall take no more brandy for a short time and thereafter, make the announcement. Does that satisfy you?"

"It does."

"Good."

Lord Kingshill immediately turned around and made to go back towards the group of four young ladies, but James caught his arm, a sudden rush of concern pushing through him.

"Wait a moment."

Lord Kingshill let out a low groan.

"Why? Whatever is the matter now?"

"I – I wondered if you would wish to go and speak with Lady Prudence for a short while *before* you make the announcement," James found himself saying, feeling both foolish and angry in equal measure. "You cannot simply go and flirt and tease those young ladies on the very same evening as you are to announce a courtship!"

"Why can I not?" Lord Kingshill frowned. "I have already made it perfectly clear to Lady Prudence that she is not to expect anything from me whether we are wed or unwed. I shall do just as I please and she will simply have to accept that." His shoulders lifted and then fell. "Therefore, I do not think it matters what I do or who I speak with."

James swallowed the tightness in his throat, aware of the rippling anger within him, but struggling to find a way to express it which would not rouse Lord Kingshill's suspicions. He could not explain why he felt so drawn to protect Lady Prudence, what it was about her that tugged her so close to him but, all the same, those feelings lingered there regardless. *That* was what had driven him when he had first seen her standing there, her fingers twisting together in nervousness, her fears about the sort of husband that Lord Kingshill was going to be more than obvious. Something within him had demanded that he care for her, demanded that he do something so that her upset would fade and thus, he had found himself promising her that he would devote himself to her and her happiness. Quite why he had said such a thing, he was still not quite sure, but nonetheless, the determination had grown all the same.

"This is not something which you need concern yourself with, my friend." Lord Kingshill chuckled and slapped James hard on the shoulder, unsettling him all the more. "Now, listen to me. This is *just* as you suggested, just as you planned, and therefore, you should be glad and contented about it! This young lady has agreed to my courtship, has agreed to marry me when the time comes and all that you need fear now is just how many young ladies you can pursue before the Season ends!"

Trying to smile, James looked away from Lord Kingshill, finding himself tense and upset. His friend was not listening to him, telling him that he had nothing whatsoever to do with his present situation and making it quite clear that he had no expectation of James' further involvement.

But I am not going to listen. I cannot, not after what I have promised Lady Prudence.

"Here, why do I not fetch you another brandy?"

Lord Kingshill looked back at James sharply, his eyebrows lifting.

"What is this? A moment ago, you told me that I ought not to touch any further liquor and now, here you are, suggesting that I take more brandy!"

James shrugged and forced his smile to stretch all the wider.

"Ah, but I have realized that I have been much too fervent," he said, making Lord Kingshill laugh aloud. "I was too concerned about outward appearances and now I realize that such things are not at all important, not when the marriage has already been agreed between yourself and Lady Prudence!"

"Precisely!" Lord Kingshill explained, slapping James on the back for the second time, his eyes lit with good humor. "Another brandy will suit me very well."

"Excellent. I will go in search of a footman. They cannot be too hard to find!"

Turning away, James made his way through the crowd, finding a footman very easily and, thereafter, returning to his friend with not only one but three glasses of brandy held very carefully in his hands.

"Three? Good gracious!"

"One is mine," James told his friend."

Lord Kingshill's eyes slanted towards the third.

"And this one?"

"Well, whoever finishes their first drink before the other may have this one," James suggested, laughing just a little as Lord Kingshill grabbed his brandy and took a large mouthful. "Though do be a little cautious, my friend, there is plenty of brandy present!"

"Ah, but for how long?" Lord Kingshill asked, his eyes sharp. "It may be that the brandy set aside for this evening will be drunk in only an hour or two and then what shall we do?" So saying, he took another mouthful and then reached for the third glass of brandy held in James' hand. "It is best to be cautious and enjoy this while we can."

"I suppose so," James agreed, having still not lifted his glass to his lips though his smile quirked all the same. "Let us hope that the evening is an exceptionally good one indeed."

～

JAMES COULD NOT HELP but nudge his friend a little, laughing inwardly when Lord Kingshill staggered so terribly that he crashed into the fence to his right.

"*Do* be careful, my friend," he grinned as Lord Kingshill fought to regain his balance. "Your carriage is only a little way over here."

"I do not know why they could not have brought it to the step," Lord Kingshill slurred, his eyes half closed as he leaned much too far the other way, forcing James to support him. "I know there are a great many guests taking their leave, but I would have thought that a Marquess would have been given priority."

"You *asked* to walk," James reminded him, a smile settling on his face as contentment rose within him. "You said that it would be no trouble, despite the fact that there were those seeking to hold you back for fear of you injuring yourself!"

"Did I?" Lord Kingshill leaned all the more into James and James was again forced to support him, attempting to hold his friend up as they finally came in sight of the waiting carriage.

James nodded.

"You did. Now, here is your carriage. Let me help you up into it." With great effort from both James and the driver, Lord Kingshill managed to get himself inside and, with a long sigh of evident relief, flopped back and leaned his head against the squabs. "Good evening, Kingshill," James called, waving one hand. "I will speak with you tomorrow, I am sure."

He waited until the carriage had pulled away and then,

with a long sigh of relief, rubbed his hands together and turned back towards the house. The evening had, to his mind, been a great success. After hearing from Lord Kingshill that he had no intention of treating Lady Prudence with even the smallest amount of kindness, he had come up with another plan and an entirely different solution.

No announcement of the courtship had been made, and that was exactly what James had wanted. Lady Prudence was not about to be embarrassed by a gentleman who cared nothing for her, and who made that more than apparent in what he said and in what he did. The idea of having Lord Kingshill make that announcement when it was clear that he had no intention of spending any time whatsoever with Lady Prudence made James' heart sink so low that he had not been able to bear it. Kingshill's attitude was so very different from how James knew himself to be, but he had not let the implications of that comparison sink deep into his thoughts. The only thing that he had wanted to do was to make certain that Lady Prudence was treated well, and not brought to any sort of further embarrassment, and thus, he had found himself acting in a way which was most unlike him. Turning on his heel, James went to walk back towards the townhouse, only to come face to face with a gentleman he had never encountered before.

"Might I enquire as to your name, sir?" The gentleman's eyes flashed, his bearded chin lifting just a little. "I have seen you speaking with my daughter and, though I believe that my wife is introduced to you, given the way that she merely watched and did not interject, I wonder if I might be granted the same privilege?"

A little perturbed by this remark, James hesitated but, seeing the gleam in the older gentleman's eye, felt very much that he simply could not refuse.

"The Marquess of Childers, sir." He inclined his head. "Forgive me, might I ask the same of you?"

The gentleman snorted.

"I suppose it is to be expected that a gentleman of your caliber would not recognize *which* young lady it is that I speak of. No doubt you have entertained many of them this evening alone!"

James scowled, his jaw jutting forward.

"I assure you, the only prolonged conversation I have had this evening has been with one young lady. Thereafter, I spent all of my time with friends and acquaintances." His eyes widened for a moment, his breath catching as he realized who this gentleman might be. "Might I guess that you are Lord Lymington?"

The gentleman's eyebrows knotted together.

"Yes. That does surprise me, I must say. I would have thought that, after all that I have heard of you, you would not know of whom I spoke. But then, mayhap on this occasion, you have done as you said, yes?"

"Yes, I did." James held his gaze without blinking, refusing to be cowed. "Might I ask why you think to speak to me? I can assure you, I did nothing to upset your daughter."

"No, you did not." Lord Lymington tilted his head, studying James in the dim light. "I must ask why you prevented your friend from announcing his courtship. I know that he had intended it to be made this evening and yet, you prevented it. I saw how you led Lord Kingshill away from the center of the ballroom, and how you encouraged him to step to the back of the room instead. He sat there, slumped in the shadows for a while, did he not?"

"Yes, he did." Unable to ascertain why this gentleman might be saying such a thing, James spread out both his hands. "You may be surprised to learn – as your daughter was also – that I am able to have concern for those other than myself. This evening, knowing that my friend was to make such an announcement, I went to speak with him." Choosing to be truthful, James dropped his hands again and shrugged. "I do not want your daughter to be embarrassed. I was the one who arranged the match, I confess, and yet I find that I am concerned that Lord Kingshill may not be taking the matter as seriously as he ought. Given that he intended to make the announcement when he was already in his cups – and, given that he did not care about what impact it would have upon your daughter either – I confess that I *did* make certain that he could not do so. As he drank more brandy, I encouraged him away from the other guests until I was finally able to encourage him to return home."

This statement was met with a long silence and James, despite his best intentions, found himself struggling to look at Lord Lymington any longer. Instead, with a clearing of his throat, he pulled his shoulders back as he clasped his hands behind his back, shuffled his feet a little, and then eventually, dropped his gaze.

"Goodness, I confess that I am most astonished – and I am not often astonished, Lord Childers."

Blinking, James lifted his head.

"I beg your pardon?"

"You have the reputation of a rogue and yet, here you are, looking after my daughter's interests as though she were your sister. I confess that, despite my uncertainty about your character, I am grateful to you for what you did this evening." Lord Lymington shook his head and then ran one hand over his chin. "I too have been watching Lord Kingshill this evening. I did not find myself pleased with his behavior nor with his complete lack of interest in my daughter." A dark scowl pulled at Lord Lymington's expression, and he shook his head again. "If she was not so determined, then I would do all that I could to make certain that she did not marry him. Though..." Coming to a slow stop, Lord Lymington frowned as though he had just realized who it was that he was speaking to. "Regardless of that, the only thing I wish to say is thank you for considering her – and for your awareness as regards the impropriety of your friend."

With a quick bow, he turned away and walked back to his own carriage, no doubt ready to take his leave with his family.

James did not move.

All that had just happened to him had made him feel so utterly astonished, it was as though every single part of his body was laden with heavy weights. He could not move, not even if he tried, for Lord Lymington's words were rushing through his mind and pushing down upon him. Was it guilt that he felt? Relief? Gladness? He could not quite make it out, closing his eyes and letting his emotions slowly begin to separate themselves, one from the other.

He felt... happy. It was the most extraordinary feeling to be appreciated, and for his good actions to be noticed. He had been determined to defend himself, a little surprised when the gentleman had accepted his words as truth. Was this what it felt like to be a respectable gentleman, held high in the esteem of others? It had been so long since he had felt himself a respectable fellow that he had quite forgotten what it felt like.

A slow but small smile began to push at the corners of his lips. Instead of being berated, instead of feeling chagrin and telling himself that he cared nothing for the consideration of others, James suddenly felt a sense of pride, as though he now stood just a fraction taller.

It was a wonderful feeling and, as James finally began to make his way back towards the townhouse, having thought to enter the ball again and enjoy a little more company, he turned quickly and instead, hailed his carriage. There was no more need for dancing, teasing, or flirtation tonight. He did not want to do such things, having already committed to Lady Prudence that he would consider *only* her for as long as it took and, besides which, had he not already embarrassed himself a great deal in front of her already?

With a nod to himself, James silently resolved to return home, praying that this sensation of appreciation and happiness would continue to linger for the next few hours at least.

CHAPTER THIRTEEN

*S*winging her leg idly, Prudence leaned her head back against the bench, letting her eyes close as the sunlight shone down upon her. She could only linger here for a few moments with the sun on her skin for fear of developing freckles, but the warmth felt good and made her smile.

"Prudence? Your mother said that you were out in the gardens." Prudence sat up quickly, rearranging her skirts as she inclined her head to her father, afraid of what he would think. "My dear girl, you need not stand on ceremony for me!" Lord Lymington chuckled and then, much to Prudence's surprise, embraced her. "I thought you did very well last evening, my dear."

"Did very well?" Prudence's eyebrows rose. "Papa, I did nothing."

He grinned at her.

"Precisely."

"I – I do not understand what you mean."

Lord Lymington tilted his head.

"I mean to say that, given the expectation, you did not appear to be nervous or even anxious when the announcement was not made. You seemed contented to return to the carriage."

"Oh." Prudence sat back down on the garden bench as her father took the one opposite her. "I did not see Lord Kingshill last evening, though I knew he was present."

Her father nodded.

"And you did not feel upset at all when the announcement was forgotten?" Leaning forward in his chair, he clicked his tongue. "You were expecting him to announce the betrothal, were you not?"

Prudence sighed.

"I was, but it seems that he chose not to do so, though I do not know why."

"That is what I wish to speak to you about, Prudence." Her father smiled at her as though to take any sort of fear away. "That gentleman was in his cups, and was much too inebriated to speak with any clarity or any consideration. Therefore, when I note that another gentleman, Lord Childers, came to speak with you and, thereafter, came to your aid, I wonder what it is that you might think of him."

"Of Lord Childers?"

Her father nodded.

"He is a scoundrel," Prudence told him, wondering if her mother had already spoken to her father about this - was he was now coming to make certain that Prudence understood? "He is a friend of Lord Kingshill, and he was the one who made possible the arrangement between us."

"And yet, be that as it may, it appears that he is rather concerned about this marriage and hopes and prays that all will go well." He reached up one hand to rub his chin. "I confess, I find that rather surprising, for a gentleman such as he. But yet, I cannot help but believe that he is genuine, given all that he did to protect you last evening."

Confused, Prudence's breath swirled in her chest.

"Protect me?"

Her father nodded.

"I watched as he spoke at length with Lord Kingshill, and saw how utterly inebriated Lord Kingshill was. The more the evening went on, the more brandy he consumed and, though I fully expected him to make the announcement, he did not."

"And he did not because of Lord Childers?"

Lord Lymington nodded.

"Precisely. Your friend took Lord Kingshill from the center of the room and pushed him back into the shadows." He held up one hand, perhaps hearing what Prudence's mind whispered. "You do not wish me to call him your friend, then. I shall call him an acquaintance instead."

"I thank you," Prudence mumbled, her face growing a little hot as she realized just how hard she found that to consider.

"He kept Lord Kingshill from making any sort of proclamation when he was so without sense," her father continued, quietly. "He even made certain to place Lord

Kingshill in his carriage so that he could not attempt to come back into the ballroom! I watched that happen and felt such a great appreciation, I could not help but speak to him."

"You did?"

Her father nodded.

"I talked with him and made it clear that I was very grateful for his consideration of you and his recognition of what the *ton* would have said, had they heard such a thing from the inebriated Lord Kingshill! He says that since he has arranged the match, he feels a responsibility and that he is now going to set his mind away from his own activities this Season until all is at an end between yourself and Lord Kingshill. Is that not remarkable?" Lord Lymington shook his head and chuckled. "From an upstanding gentleman, I might not be surprised, but for a rogue... it was most extraordinary to hear such words from his lips! And given what I witnessed, I had no reason to doubt him."

A thrill ran up Prudence's spine upon hearing all of this, only for her mother's warnings to come back to her mind. She dared not let her father see all that she felt, for fear that he would question her further – asking questions which she did not have answers for.

"That is remarkable indeed, but he is still a scoundrel, Papa, as Mother has reminded me."

To her surprise, Lord Lymington did not immediately answer and certainly did not instantly agree. Instead, he mused for a few moments, his gaze drifting away from her as Prudence found herself waiting urgently for what judgment he might bring upon Lord Childers. For whatever reason, it seemed to matter a great deal to her what her father thought of Lord Childers, and she wondered silently if her father would urge her to stay away from Lord Childers, just as her mother had done.

"You are correct that he still has the reputation of a rogue," Lord Lymington agreed, after a few moments. "However, I do not think that, in this situation, he is acting as one. It seems to me that Lord Childers is genuinely interested in making certain that all is well – though that might very well be because his friend is involved and he feels partly responsible, given that he was the one who made the match."

Prudence looked down at her hands, twisting her fingers in her lap as a slow joy began to burst up from within her.

"That is good of you to say, Papa." She dared a glance at him, praying that he could not see within her heart and know what was hidden there. "Might I ask if I ought to refrain from his company, however?"

Again, her father paused but, this time, there was a light smile on his face as he thought.

"No, I do not think so," came the eventual reply. "If Lord Childers proves himself to be your guide in this – though I think that he does it all for the sake of his reputation – then you can continue on in his company at present. Though, if he should return to his rakish ways, I will immediately pull you from his company and nothing more will be heard of him." A severe heaviness sank into his expression, his smile fading. "Do you understand me, Prudence?"

"I do, Papa. You are very clear on the matter, and I

greatly appreciate it." Prudence managed to smile, relieved when her father rose to his feet. He had given her a good deal to think about and now she wanted to be able to do that in silence and alone. "I thank you for sharing that with me."

Her father walked towards her, leaned over, and dropped a kiss on her forehead.

"You are a very dear daughter, Prudence," he said softly, looking down into her face. "You need not fear the past, nor be concerned for your future. I am here to both guide and support you, as is your mother. I will not set you wrong in this, though I must also have *your* trust so that if anything Lord Childers does or says is improper, you will step back from his company at once and inform me of it."

Prudence looked up at her father, seeing the way that he searched her face.

"I shall, Papa," she swore, reaching up to take his hand for a moment. "Will you tell Mama of this also?"

"I go to speak with her at this very moment," he smiled, as Prudence released his hand. "Excuse me."

Watching him leave, Prudence then turned her head and, after a moment, dropped it into her hands. She closed her eyes tightly and dragged in air, her heart pounding in a way that she had managed to keep hidden from her father.

Lord Childers told me that he would be devoted to my betrothal, to making certain that all was well, and I was contented. But I did not think that he would ever do something like this!

"I do not know what to think, I confess it."

"Nor do I," Prudence answered, passing one hand over her eyes. "It was the most extraordinary thing to have heard from my father. I admit, when I first heard Lord Childers speak such words, when he first told me that he would be devoted to my happiness in my upcoming betrothal, I did not know what to think. I did not fully believe him, I suppose. For why should a gentleman, such as he, care about anything to do with me?"

Miss Rockwell shook her head, her brows furrowing as she looked at Prudence.

"I do not know," she said again, digging her spoon into the ice they had both just purchased from Gunther's. "That is most extraordinary. Do you truly think that he will be devoted to this, as he has said?"

Prudence shrugged.

"It seems as though he might be, given what he did. My father seemed... pleased."

Miss Rockwell's eyebrows shot high.

"Pleased?"

"Yes," Prudence admitted, her mouth twisting to one side for a moment. "He seemed rather taken with the fact that Lord Childers had done such a thing. I did see that Lord Kingshill was a little overcome with liquor at the ball and... well, I was relieved when no announcement was made."

Her friend smiled sympathetically as Prudence took a mouthful of her ice.

"I can understand that. Are you still quite certain that you wish to marry him?"

Prudence took a deep breath and then let it out slowly. She knew that she could be honest with her friend and yet, inwardly, something held her back.

"I must marry him if I am to have any hope of a satisfactory future."

"But not a happy one? What of that?"

Taking a breath, Prudence set her shoulders and tried to speak plainly.

"My dear friend, I greatly value our friendship, but it will not last forever, will it? Not in this way, at least, for you will soon marry and go to set up home at your husband's estate. I shall be left alone and, if I do not marry, then I will only have my mother and father for company for as many years as God grants them. What then? Must I become a spinster aunt to whatever nieces and nephews I have? What will happen when they grow, and my sister desires her own house to be filled with simply her own family? I do not say that I will be destitute, but that I shall certainly be unfulfilled and lonely. Is that any sort of future for a young lady such as myself?"

A long sigh came from Miss Rockwell.

"Well, when you speak in such terms as that, I can understand why you are so concerned. But does it have to be Lord Kingshill?"

A small, sad smile touched Prudence's lips.

"I do not know who else it would be, Anna. It is not as though any gentlemen have come in search of me, is it? And no one knows that I am betrothed as yet, so I cannot use that as an excuse."

Miss Rockwell's lips tugged to one side, only for her eyes to flare and her spoon to drop to the table. She did not even glance at it, did not stop to pick it up but instead reached out to touch Prudence's hand with her own.

"What about Lord Childers?"

"What do you mean?" Prudence could not deny that her heart quickened a little at that name, but she steeled herself inwardly. "What about him?"

"Could you not betrothe yourself to Lord Childers?" Miss Rockwell's eyes widened all the more. "He has said that he will devote himself to you, has he not?"

"Yes, but to ensure the betrothal that follows is a happy one."

"Which speaks of his interest in you, does it not?"

Prudence blinked and then shook her head, her lips pursed for a moment.

"I do not think that it means that he has any sort of genuine interest, not in that regard. He says that he feels it only because of his hand in the arrangement, not for any other reason."

"But regardless of that, he is proving himself to be a little more reformed than Lord Kingshill, is he not? And your father seemed pleased with him."

"Yes," Prudence said slowly, wishing that her heart was not so eager to cling to this particular idea, given the way it jumped around. "But I could not dare to suggest such a thing to him! He does not want to marry, while his friend does. What if–"

"What if you miss this opportunity and instead, find yourself tied to Lord Kingshill for the rest of your days, wondering what would have happened, had you been bold enough to speak with Lord Childers?"

Prudence swallowed thickly, her stomach lurching. Was this what would happen to her if she did *not* do as Miss Rockwell suggested? She could not help but admit to herself that the thought of marrying Lord Childers was a good deal more appealing than the idea of attaching herself to Lord Kingshill, though she did her best to hide that from her friend.

"I will think about it, Anna. That is all I can say."

Miss Rockwell nodded.

"Then think on it quickly, my friend. It will not be long before Lord Kingshill makes his announcement about your courtship, and then what will the *ton* do if they see you connected to Lord Childers instead?" Picking up her spoon, she dug it into her ice again. "I think that Lord Childers might be the better prospect, even though he is just as much of a rogue as Lord Kingshill!"

"Perhaps," Prudence mused, seeing her friend nod fervently. "I do not know how I would even approach such a subject, however!"

"It will come to you, I am sure," Miss Rockwell said, firmly. "I am *very* glad that I thought of such a thing." Reaching out, she pressed Prudence's hand, her eyes steady. "I want you to be happy, my dear friend. I cannot bear the thought of you being wed to that *fool* and left unhappy for the rest of your days."

A sense of sadness twisted Prudence's heart and then spread out across her chest.

"I do not want to be sorrowful either," she answered, as Miss Rockwell took her hand back. "I *will* think about it, I assure you. I will think about speaking to Lord Childers about changing my betrothal from Lord Kingshill to him."

CHAPTER FOURTEEN

"*I* shall make the announcement this evening, I think."

James looked at his friend, frowning.

"You mean to speak to everyone at this soiree?" He looked around the room as his friend nodded. "But Lady Prudence is not here this evening."

"Does she have to be?" Lord Kingshill snorted and shook his head. "Come now, do not be so foolish as to tell me that the lady herself must be in the same room when I make the announcement!"

"I think it would be wise to make certain that the lady is present before you make such a big announcement," James answered, quickly. "The *ton* will expect to see you together and–"

"I do not care what the *ton* think, or what their expectations are." Lord Kingshill interrupted, rolling his eyes. "And there was a time when you did not either." Tilting his head, he narrowed his eyes and looked long at James.

"There is something different about you of late, I must say. I do not know exactly what it is, but there is certainly something strange. You are not the friend that I once knew, I think."

"There is nothing different about me," James stated, firmly. "You are mistaken there, I assure you."

His friend spread out his hands.

"Then why so concerned about what the *ton* will say or think?"

"Because... because I think you lack wisdom here," James faltered, though he drew himself up to stand tall. "It is as though you care nothing for the lady, nor for the reputation which she will soon be tied to. Do you not think of the future? Do you not think of your heirs? Surely you will want the very best for them, and the very best means that you must think of all that you are doing at this present moment."

"Pshaw!" Lord Kingshill flung up his hands. "You are speaking foolishness! You know very well that I am just as much a rogue as you, and that I have no intention of changing my ways. That is the very reason that you created this match between myself and Lady Prudence, so that I might continue in my ways without any worry or concern over my future. Now, however, it appears to me as though you are quite determined for me to *change* so that the *ton* and my bride-to-be – once we are betrothed – think better of me. That is very strange, my friend."

"Mayhap I have seen things as they really are," James answered, refusing to permit even the smallest murmur of affection for Lady Prudence to show in his voice or his expression. "Mayhap I have realized that there is more to our responsibilities than merely producing an heir."

Lord Kingshill reeled back as though James had struck him.

"Do you mean to say that you, yourself, have determined to turn your back on all that we have enjoyed together these last few years? That you intend to become dull and staid?"

James waved a hand.

"No, of course not."

"Then what are you saying?"

Pausing, James tried to find an answer, one that he could give which would satisfy his friend's questions, but nothing came. Instead, he simply cleared his throat and shrugged, looking away from Lord Kingshill.

"I am not sure yet."

"Goodness." Lord Kingshill passed one hand over his eyes. "I did not think that such a thing would ever happen." His hand fell to his side. "I did not think that I would ever see this. I did not think that I would ever witness my friend turning away from such enjoyments. You are determined, I think, to become a respectable gentleman rather than a scandalous one, and I wish I could understand why." He shook his head. "Our friendship is altered forever now, I fear."

"No, it is not." James tried to cast aside all that had been said of him, tried to pretend that none of what his friend had stated was in the least bit true, but his heart told him otherwise. It held fast to Lady Prudence, telling him that the only reason he wanted to better himself, the only reason that he wanted to improve his character and his standing was because of her. He could not hide it from himself.

But I can hide it from him.

"Mayhap I have just become a little bored," he stated, shrugging his shoulders lightly and looking away. "There is no excitement, no adventure any longer. I have ladies pursuing *me* now, so I have never any requirement to chase after them."

"So instead, you have determined that being a respectable fellow is better?" Lord Kingshill sneered, his eyes a little sharp, but James quickly nodded. "For whose benefit?"

"For my own," James answered, clearly. "Now, you need not say that our friendship is at an end, or altered in any way, for we are still aligned in many ways. It does not mean that I am going to change entirely, only that I am going to be a little more careful in whom I keep company with."

"And you desire that *I* should become a little more respectable also, for some reason."

"For Lady Prudence's sake, yes." Choosing to be honest, James held his friend's gaze. "You cannot make the announcement when she is not present. It would not be fair to her – and she might well then decide to cancel the arrangement before you even begin courting!"

With a heavy sigh, Lord Kingshill shrugged his shoulders.

"Very well. I will wait until either she arrives, or we are at another social occasion together. There now, does that satisfy you?"

James tried to say yes, tried to feel a sense of pleasure

and hope, but instead all there was within his heart was a great sense of dismay and disappointment. Yes, there was relief that no announcement was being made as yet, but that was not filling him with any sort of happiness. Could it be as Lord Kingshill said? Was he truly going to become dull and staid if he did not continue in his roguish ways? And what would happen when Lady Prudence *did* marry Lord Kingshill? Would he feel even the smallest gladness for them? Or would there be instead, as he feared, this very same disappointment and dismay which, in time, would grow to be the heaviest burden he had ever carried?

James meandered slowly through the park, walking along familiar paths but finding no happiness or peace of mind as he did so. The early morning meant that he had no other companions with him and there were very few others – if anyone – there but that was just as James wanted it. There was so much on his mind, and in his heart, that he could not help but seek out some sort of respite.

The cool morning air did nothing to aid him in that. Neither did the soft morning birdsong, the sweet scent of the flowers in the air, or the beauty of the grounds that surrounded him.

His heart was too heavy for all of that.

Twice now, he had stopped Lord Kingshill from announcing that he was now courting Lady Prudence with the intention of it leading to a betrothal. Twice now, he had stepped forward and placed himself directly into the path of his friend, holding him back and making certain that what his friend had *wanted* to say was not pronounced. Yes, he had told himself, he had wished to make quite certain that all went well as regards the betrothal, and that Lady Prudence was contented, but where had that desire come from? When he had first suggested Lord Kingshill, he had not cared a jot about the lady in question! Now, however, he found himself determined to take the best care of her that he could.

There was only one answer for that.

Dropping his head, James let out a long groan as he rubbed one hand over his eyes. There was a true, genuine *affection* in his heart for Lady Prudence and that, to him, was the very worst of things. How could he have let his heart feel such a thing as that? How could he have let himself become so close to her, so involved with her that he no longer wanted to behave in any sort of roguish manner? The time that she had witnessed him beckoning another young lady close – even though he had been rejected – had burned into his mind with such a fierceness, it was hard to even think of it without snatching in a breath. The mortification stung at his soul, even though he had done such a thing many a time before, without even the smallest hint of guilt.

It was all because of her.

James stopped, rubbed one hand down his face again, and let out another long breath. This was not at all what he had wanted. He had never set out with the intention of letting his heart fill with a tenderness for the young lady his friend was to court. Yet, his heart had been so determined, it had dragged him to a new situation, and a new set of circumstances where the thought of stepping away from Lady Prudence, of seeing her wed to Lord Kingshill, made James feel almost physically unwell.

I must stop this.

The thought had him lifting his head, sharply. What did he mean by such a thing? Was it that he thought of stopping his own heart from continuing to build an affection for her? Or was it that he wanted to stop the connection between Lord Kingshill and Lady Prudence from growing?

Taking a deep breath, James set his shoulders and continued to walk through the park, his brow furrowing and his chin dropping forward. He did not know what it was that he meant. He did not even know what it was that he wanted. Myriad thoughts were plaguing his mind, tormenting him with every step he took. He could not be free of them... and perhaps did not *want* to be free of them either.

"Oh, excuse me!"

James stumbled, his head lifting sharply as a figure darted to one side, barely missing knocking into him. He blinked, stopping in his walk as he turned, an apology ready on his lips. His head had been down, he had not looked ahead of him and mayhap, whoever this was had been doing the same and simply had not seen him approach.

"Forgive me, I–" A strangled sound came from his throat as he looked into the very face of the person he had been thinking about. "Lady Prudence! Whatever are you doing here?"

She glanced away from him before looking back again, appearing a little nervous.

"I was simply walking," she said, softly. "Pray, do not tell anyone that you have seen me, for I ought to have a chaperone but... " Her eyes closed for a moment. "I needed a few minutes alone."

"I understand, and I would never say a word, I assure you." Her eyes caught his and James smiled in what he hoped was a comforting way. "We find ourselves in the same situation, I think."

Her eyebrows lifted, her curls dancing lightly at her temples.

"Oh?"

He nodded.

"I am walking in the hope of clearing the many thoughts which are presently running through my mind," he said, quietly. "Might I surmise that this is your trouble also?"

She looked at him for a long moment before she nodded.

"Yes."

"I see."

Lady Prudence pressed her lips together, then spread out her hands.

"Might I ask what it is that you are thinking about? What it is that torments you so?"

A sudden fire lit up James' heart and he snatched a breath, turning his head so that he did not have to look at her. A fierce hope began to burn through him, begging – nay, demanding – that he tell her the truth.

"Ah, Lady Prudence," he said, softly, still unable to

bring his gaze back to hers. "My thoughts, my tormenting, difficult, struggling thoughts, are centered on one thing and one thing alone." With an effort, he forced himself to look back into her face, seeing the question in her green eyes. "My dear Lady Prudence, they are focused entirely upon you."

CHAPTER FIFTEEN

I *am well and truly awake.*

With a scowl, Prudence lay as still as she could, her eyes still closed but no sense of tiredness came to her. Instead, only wakefulness pursued, demanding that she rise and greet the day even though, to her mind, it was much too early.

This is foolishness, she told herself, firmly, keeping her eyes closed. *I cannot ask Lord Childers to marry me instead of Lord Kingshill. That could make these difficult circumstances all the more intolerable.*

After all that she and Miss Rockwell had discussed, Prudence had not been able to give herself even a single moment of rest. The thought of speaking to Lord Childers and asking if *he* might be the gentleman that she could wed, instead of Lord Kingswell, was both terrifying and wonderful at the same time. There was a great fear there, of course, a fear that Lord Childers would laugh at her and refuse her request, should she even have the courage to ask him such a thing but, at the same time, there was a great hope which continued to build within her heart. A hope that she would find a happiness which, thus far, had evaded her entirely, should she have the boldness to ask him such a thing.

But if I ask him and he refuses, then I shall be left with nothing but a broken heart and a deep, relentless pain that will never leave me. Is it worth asking him such a thing, knowing what might wait for me in his answer?

Sighing to herself, Prudence rose from her bed and dressed quickly, knowing that it was far too early for the maids to appear. The questions continued to buzz around her mind and though she tried to swat them away, they simply would not leave. There was an affection in her heart for Lord Childers, she knew, though she very much wished that it would take its leave of her! It did not do as she asked, nor as she hoped, however, but instead, continued to grow and press out into the very furthermost reaches of her heart. Was what Miss Rockwell said right? Was there a genuine interest in Lord Childers heart for her? Or was he simply doing as he felt he ought to do, given that he had made the arrangement for the match so far?

With another heartfelt sigh, Prudence splashed some water on her face and, after a few moments, went to the door. She stepped out carefully into the hallway, praying that no one would see her. Soon, the maid would come, and she would have to give an explanation – but she could simply say she had been in the gardens rather than out walking alone. On tiptoes, Prudence made her way out of doors, breathing in the crisp morning air and quickly making her way to the park.

IT WAS A BEAUTIFUL DAY, she considered, ambling along the path with her head tilted a little bit upwards so that she might be able to see the sky. The sun had already risen, and though the air was a little chilled, it was not cold enough for her to shiver. She let herself smile softly, though that smile did not last long. Her thoughts returned to Lord Childers and all that Miss Rockwell had suggested and, as she thought of him, her heart leaped with a sudden fierceness that caught her breath and stole it away for a moment.

To be thinking of him in such a way was, to her mind, still nothing but foolishness and yet, all the same, the thoughts and the emotions within her lingered. That was what she wanted, if she was honest with herself. She *wanted* to be close to him, wanted to pull herself towards him, rather than toward Lord Kingshill. The idea of betrothing herself to Lord Kingshill when her heart was betraying her seemed wrong, somehow, as though she would be disloyal to herself by doing such a thing.

So will I speak to him, then? Her eyes closed for a moment as she gave a quick, sharp shake of her head, opening them again only to see a gentleman only a step away, his own head lowered. With an exclamation of surprise, she jerked out of his path, her heart pounding suddenly.

"Forgive me!" the gentleman exclaimed, turning to look at her.

His eyes widened, just as her own breath caught again, one hand flying to her heart as she looked into

Lord Childers' face. What was he doing out walking in the park at such an early hour? Did not gentlemen such as he remain abed until at least noon, recovering from whatever it was that they had engaged in the night before?

Lord Childers blinked in obvious surprise.

"Lady Prudence! Whatever are you doing here?"

"I was simply walking," she answered, a sudden fear clutching at her heart. After all, she was out here alone and a young lady such as herself ought to have a chaperone. She knew Lord Childers' reputation, of course, and still did not fear that he would do anything improper, but all the same, she feared that he might tell someone else that he had seen her here alone, in the early hours of the morning, and her reputation would be severely damaged thereafter. "Pray, do not tell anyone that you have seen me, for I ought to have a chaperone but… " She closed her eyes for a moment. "I needed a few minutes alone."

"I understand, and I would never say a word, I assure you." Prudence looked back at him, a little surprised, though she said nothing. "We find ourselves in the very same situation, I think."

Immediately, questions began to rise in her mind, though Prudence only tipped her head just a little, wondering if he would respond badly to her questioning him on what such a thing might be.

"Oh?"

After a moment, Lord Childers nodded, his mouth tugging lightly to one side for just a moment.

"I am walking in the hope of clearing the many thoughts which are presently running through my mind."

His eyes searched hers. "Might I surmise that this is your trouble also?"

Dare I speak of what it is that I have been thinking of? Lacking the courage for more, Prudence managed a brief smile, but only one word.

"Yes."

"I see."

She looked at him, seeing the way that his eyebrows furrowed, sending lines across his forehead. Dare she ask him about what was on his mind? Mayhap if he was willing to share such things with her, she might then find the courage to respond with the same honesty. Taking a deep breath, she spread out her hands.

"Might I ask what it is that you are thinking about? What it is that torments you so?"

Instantly, Lord Childers turned his head away, his jaw tight as he gazed across the park. Prudence wanted to apologize, to tell him that she ought not to have been questioning him so, and that he did not really need to answer, only for him to sigh and then begin to speak.

"Ah, Lady Prudence," he responded quietly, a softness in his voice which spoke of pain. "My thoughts, my tormenting, difficult, struggling thoughts, are centered on one thing and one thing alone." Wondering at this, Prudence held his gaze as he looked back at her, her own heart beating a little more quickly such was the anticipation within her heart. What would send a rogue out to the park in the early hours of the morning? Why would he be out here walking alone? Lord Childers licked his lips and then put out one hand in her direction. "My dear Lady Prudence, they are focused entirely upon you."

The words ran into her mind and then went straight to her heart, her own emotions flaring hot. She swallowed tightly, wondering at them, only to then douse her fiery hopes. This was, no doubt, just another part of his determination to make certain that her betrothal to Lord Kingshill went as well as it could. He had arranged the match and now felt responsible. That was all.

"You are very kind," she said, not quite certain what else to say. "I am sure that all will go well once Lord Kingshill makes the announcement about our courtship."

"Which has not yet happened."

Prudence's breath clattered in her chest as Lord Childers took a step closer to her, his eyes suddenly vivid, deep, and intense all at the same time as he gazed down into her face.

"Our courtship?" she managed to say, her voice squeaking out of her. "No, not as yet."

"And thus, there can be no betrothal, not yet anyway." She shook her head, looking back into his eyes but saying nothing. The gentle breeze drifted around her, reminding her gently of where she was, and that she had no chaperone, but Prudence ignored the reminder easily enough. Her stomach twisted this way and that as silence grew between them though Lord Childers did not once even glance away from her. It was as though he were determined to either unnerve her or have her open her mouth to confess the truth to him about her own heart. She blinked, swallowed, and then let out a slow breath and, at this, Lord Childers immediately dropped his head and ran one hand over his eyes. "Forgive me. I am being too forward and I–"

"Why are your thoughts about me?"

The moment that she said those words, Prudence's face burned with embarrassment, and she quickly looked away, stammering an apology – only for Lord Childers to take her hand. The action was startling enough to have her look back at him directly, seeing the tiniest smile tugging at the corner of his lips.

"I will tell you if you wish it."

She took another breath, trying to settle the way that her whole body now seemed to be jumping and shaking and shivering all at once.

"If you are concerned about my betrothal to Lord Kingshill, though it has not come about yet, then–"

"It is not about your connection to Lord Kingshill." Lord Childers then shook his head, pressing her hand a little. "That is to say, it *is* about that in some ways, though it is not the primary reason for my thoughts and my confusion. The reason I say this, Lady Prudence, is because I do not want you to misunderstand."

"Then please, do share the truth with me."

Her voice was breathless, her stomach twisting hard as she fought to keep her gaze steady. There was something significant here, she could tell. Something momentous which they were both about to stumble into, should he be bold enough to tell her and should she be willing enough to hear it. She could barely take in a breath, her chest tight as her fingers gripped his a little more.

"I shall." Lord Childers frowned, then, rubbing one hand over his chin he paused, perhaps trying to find the right words to say. "Lady Prudence, the truth is that, while I am concerned about your connection to Lord

Kingshill, I never once expected to have such concerns. In truth, I believed that I was doing it all to make certain that my friend could have what he desired, without putting too much difficulty in his path."

"Difficulty?"

Lord Childers' mouth flattened, and he shook his head again.

"The truth is, Lady Prudence, that Lord Kingshill has never expressed a desire to change his ways." He pressed her hand again and then dropped it, leaving her feeling suddenly cold. "What he wanted was to continue in this roguish manner, while, at the same time, having a wife and an heir produced. And I, being his friend and unwilling to lose his friendship and the camaraderie we shared, thought I would do what I could to help him."

A chill began to creep over Prudence's skin.

"You mean to say that you arranged this match, knowing that the lady Lord Kingshill married would be subjected to these great and difficult trials that no doubt come with being wed to a scoundrel?"

Dropping his head still lower, Lord Childers nodded.

"Yes, that is the truth."

She took a step back from him, her whole body shaking now, rather violently.

"I did not know – I thought that..."

"I made you believe it all," he confessed, looking up at her again. "I wanted you to be quite contented in the arrangement, for what was nothing more than a selfish reason. But as I continued in our connection, Lady Prudence, I found that the desire within my heart was no longer for my own satisfaction, nor even for my friend to be able to continue just as he is, but rather for you."

She shook her head, her throat aching as tears began to build behind her eyes.

"I cannot marry him. I cannot let myself–"

"I do not want you to." His hand found hers again, then the other so that both of her hands were clasped tightly in his. Prudence could not look at him, shaking her head and blinking furiously in the hope of keeping her tears pressed behind her eyes. "Lady Prudence, please. Give me just another moment to explain and then I shall let you go." Swallowing hard, Prudence shook her head again but did not resist him, did not pull her hands out of his and step away.

Despite the pain in her heart, despite the harsh realization which had hit her about Lord Childers' motivations in bringing her to Lord Kingshill, there was still something about being close to him, about having her hands in his which she could not bear to step away from. Not yet at least.

"Just a moment, I beg of you," he murmured, his voice a little quieter now. "The reason that I say I do not want you to marry Lord Kingshill is because I do not think that I could bear it. Though I set out to bring you and Lord Kingshill together, I quickly discovered that what I thought I wanted was precisely the opposite of my desire. The more time that I have spent in your company, the more I have learned just how wonderful a person you are, just how beautiful your character is, and how much I desire to be in your company. You have begun to capture me, Lady Prudence, and I cannot imagine the pain which would tear through me, should you then step into Lord Kingshill's arms."

The tears which had burned behind her eyes now began to flow down Prudence's cheeks and Lord Childers, his eyes flaring wide in evident horror, pulled his hand from hers to find a handkerchief. Accepting it, Prudence wiped at her cheeks carefully, struggling to know how to respond, what she ought to say, and just what this declaration now meant.

"You – you are still a rogue."

"Yes, I am." Lord Childers put his free hand to his heart. "But I swear to you, I am reforming. You may not believe me, and I understand why you would not, but when I confessed to you that I was devoted to making certain that you were happy, there was only one reason for it." His eyes softened, his expression gentling as Prudence's heart leaped, pulling back her tears. "It is because I have come to care for you."

Prudence did not know what to say, her words twisting in her chest and refusing to come to her lips. She swallowed once, twice, then handed Lord Childers back his handkerchief. He took it and, as their fingers brushed, Prudence's heart cried out with what she knew to be both hope and happiness.

"Do you mean what you said?" she asked, as Lord Childers nodded fervently. "That night, I saw you with–"

"I told Lord Kingshill that I was struggling with my heart as regarded a particular young lady," he inter-rupted, gently, "and his advice was to pursue another young lady entirely so that I could be free of the first."

Prudence's eyes widened in understanding, her fingers now tightening around his.

"You tried to forget about me?"

"I *have* tried, and I have failed," he whispered, his nearness to her now making her skin prickle with anticipation. "I want to take Lord Kingshill's place, Prudence. I do not know what you would think of that, nor what your father or mother would state but–"

"I will ask them."

She flushed hot but did not look away, her eagerness seeming to surprise him, given the way that his eyebrows lifted. Then, he smiled and, after a moment, nodded.

"That is good. Then I shall speak to Lord Kingshill."

Prudence looked up at him again, her smile beginning to lift the corners of her mouth.

"You will?"

"Of course I shall." Lord Childers laughed and lifted his shoulders in a small shrug. "I am sure that he will have no difficulty in agreeing to it all. He does not truly want to marry anyway, I am afraid!"

Wincing, Prudence shook her head.

"I am grateful to know the truth."

"I am sorry for what I said, and the part I had to play in deceiving you there," he told her, his voice holding a tenderness which she had never heard before. "It was wrong of me, and I ought never to have done it."

"It is forgotten." A sudden thought came to her, reminding her of her own past and whether or not she ought to tell him the truth about her foolishness, though she quickly dismissed the thought. It had no bearing on this present moment and, after all, he had done a good deal more than that, she was sure! "You will speak to him soon?"

"Just as soon as I am able." Lord Childers then took her hand and, lifting it, pressed it to his lips. The kiss that he placed upon it was light but sent a heat racing down her arm and into her heart, making her tremble. "I would stay and speak to you a little longer, Lady Prudence, but I think that for your reputation's sake, I should take my leave." Releasing her hand, he bowed respectfully. "I do hope to speak to you again later today."

"I hope so too." Prudence smiled, watching him take his leave of her, pressing one hand lightly against her stomach to calm herself just a little. Even in how he had taken his leave of her, she realized, he had shown himself to be a gentleman. He had not taken advantage of her, had not sought to kiss her or wrap her in his arms – even though, were she truthful, Prudence would have given in a little too easily had he tried to do such a thing! He had been respectful, considerate, and appropriate and even that was a joy to her heart.

"I should return home," Prudence told herself, turning and, rather reluctantly, making her way back toward the edge of the park.

She glanced over her shoulder as though she hoped that he had found the separation from her too great to bear and wanted instead to see her again, but there was nothing but grass and trees to catch her eye. With a small, soft smile, Prudence made her way back to the house, feeling a great deal of happiness for the first time that Season.

CHAPTER SIXTEEN

hat is this that I am feeling? Frowning to himself as he entered the ballroom, James considered the present emotions swirling through his chest. There was not the anticipation of finding some beautiful young lady who he might pull into his arms, nor was there the hope of drinking the finest brandy and earning himself a nice pile of winnings. And yet, all the same, he felt... happy. Indeed, there was a joy within his heart that he could not quite explain, and he found himself at a loss as to why he could feel so much delight when he was going to indulge in none of what would otherwise have been his favorite pastimes.

His eyes flickered around the room as he walked, finding himself unwilling to stop and talk to anyone, though many greeted him. Yes, he nodded and smiled but he did not stop to talk, trying to understand this new state of both mind and heart. Was it simply because of Lady Prudence? Could his happiness really come from the connection between them which, through one simple yet honest conversation, had blossomed into something he had never experienced before?

A smile caught the edge of his lips, and he held his head a little higher, feeling himself thrilled at this new realization. At the same time, another thought came into his mind and his shoulders immediately dropped. He was, after all, still a rogue with a dreadful reputation, and why, then, should someone like him deserve a beautiful creature such as Lady Prudence? Surely there should be consequences for a fellow like him, the consequences being that he would never find someone who truly cared for him.

Though she has not admitted to such a thing as yet, James reminded himself, still frowning. *However, I was certain that I saw something in her eyes and heard something in her voice which hinted at the same sort of feeling within my own heart.*

That made him smile again, his heart quickening at the thought of seeing Lady Prudence again. He would not say anything to anyone as regards his intention to court her, not as yet, for there was still a conversation to have with Lord Kingshill. That, however, could be done tonight and, as he had said to Lady Prudence, he did not think there would be any difficulty there. Lord Kingshill could easily find another young lady to marry and produce the required heir though, this time, James was determined to have nothing to do with it. He had been dishonest once and he was not about to be so again. Not when he realized the injury that could be caused by it.

Besides which, he mused, his hands behind his back now as he walked, *I am sure that Lord Kingshill will be able to find someone who is more than suitable for him and, mayhap, someone who is just like him in character. Someone who has no interest in sharing their life with him, someone who would rather keep him at arm's length. Yes, there certainly must be some young lady like that!*

"Childers, good evening."

James turned as a heavy hand settled on his shoulder.

"Kingshill!" he exclaimed, a broad smile on his face. "I was just thinking of you."

His friend lifted an eyebrow.

"All good, I promise."

"That is good." Lord Kingshill lifted his half-filled brandy glass. "This is exceptional brandy, I must say."

James rolled his eyes.

"The ball has not even properly begun, and you are half in your cups already!"

"But it is such *fine* brandy!"

With a laugh, James slapped his friend hard on the back, then tilted his head.

"There is something I should like to discuss with you, however, before you become too inebriated. Might you be able to spare me a few minutes?"

Lord Kingshill frowned.

"If you are going to give me another lecture on how I ought to be doing this or that before I make my announcement, then I have no time nor inclination to listen to it."

James grinned.

"It is not that, I assure you. Rather, it is something of the opposite, though not entirely."

His friend's eyebrows lifted.

"Well, now I am intrigued!" He threw back the rest of his brandy and, smacking his lips, looked at James. "What is it?"

"Well, I should like to talk to you about Lady Prudence." A knot tied itself in his stomach as he spoke, but he kept his gaze steady. "Something has happened, and I should like to... well, I do not think that you should proceed with your betrothal."

The grin on his friend's face began to fade.

"Whatever do you mean by that? Is there something wrong with the lady? Have you discovered something about her which will not suit?"

James shook his head.

"No, no, nothing like that. However, I have considered that, while the match may be suitable for you, it is certainly not suitable for her. Think about this, my dear friend. She wants nothing more than to have by her side a gentleman who cares for her, who will give her the attention and the affection that she so craves. Do you really believe that you can provide that?"

Lord Kingshill scoffed at once.

"Of course not! But then again, I should not even think to do such things as that."

"So you can see, then, that you are not well matched."

This brought a heavy line to his friend's forehead.

"But Lady Prudence will simply have to accept that from me. She will have to understand that there can be no connection between us in the way that she desires, that is all."

The way his friend spoke, so carelessly and without the least bit of consideration for Lady Prudence, made

James' heart fill with anger, though he forced it to remain in the very depths of him so that it did not express itself either in word or in his expression.

"I do not think that she wishes for that sort of connection, Kingshill. Thus, the attachment cannot continue as anticipated."

Lord Kingshill blinked, his frown lifting.

"You mean to say that she will not proceed with this betrothal?"

James shook his head.

"No, she will not."

"But why? It is not as though she is going to be given any other gentleman's hand, is it? She is a wallflower, has been for some time, and as yet, has not garnered even the least bit of attention from anyone! Why then would she be so bold as to do this?"

The knot in James' stomach tightened but he did not hold himself back.

"Because she has received a better offer, my friend. An offer from a gentleman who has promised to be considerate, caring, and affectionate, which is just as she deserves."

Lord Kingshill snorted.

"Then she has received an offer from a pauper, I am sure. No gentleman of good standing would consider a wallflower, no matter how highly she is titled."

"He is not a pauper." James swallowed tightly, then lifted his chin. "My friend, *I* am the gentleman who has offered such a thing." His friend blinked furiously, his face paling as James swallowed the nervousness tightening his throat. "I may be just as much of a rogue as you, but I am determined to reform," he continued, before his friend could speak. "It may be the most astonishing thing you have heard, but I confess that I cannot help but care for the lady. I do not know what it is that has drawn me to her but, the more time that I have spent in her company, the more time I have *wanted* to spend there. She is a beautiful creature, her character remarkable, and her nature nothing but sweetness." Putting one hand to his heart, James inclined his head. "I am sorry to have stepped in where I ought not to have done, but as I have said, I could not help it. I *had* to be the one who came to stand by her side."

Lord Kingshill said nothing for some moments and then, much to James' astonishment, he began to laugh. The sound was cruel and hard as though he were mocking James for some reason, berating him for what he had chosen to do.

"You?" he asked, as James folded his arms over his chest, feeling a little irritated at his friend's response. "*You*, the scoundrel, the rake, the rogue... you are to marry Lady Prudence in my place... and she has accepted you?" He laughed again, though there was a darkness to his tone. "I cannot believe that."

"It is true," James insisted, firmly. "I cannot bear the thought of you taking the lady as your wife and then treating her as though she has no bearing upon your life, showing her no respect or consideration. My conscience will not permit it." Taking a deep breath, he dropped his hands. "And though I said I would assist you in finding a young lady to marry and provide you with the heir that you require, I am afraid that I cannot do so now."

"No?" Lord Kingshill's lips twisted. "No doubt your newfound conscience will not permit you to do such a thing?"

"Precisely." James drew himself up so he stood as tall as he could. "You may not believe me, you may mock and tease me, but I am determined to reform myself for *her* sake."

"And what if I refuse?"

James blinked.

"Refuse what?"

"Refuse to step away. Refuse to step *back*."

Shrugging, James turned his face away.

"It does not matter," he answered, quietly. "The lady will not marry you, Kingshill. Her father and mother have been informed of the change and they have consented." He was not certain of this last statement as yet, but he spoke it with confidence regardless. He did not want to let Lord Kingshill have even the smallest amount of belief that Lady Prudence would be to him as he had previously anticipated. "That is all there is to it."

Lord Kingshill scowled, his eyes growing dark, his jaw jutting forward.

"You devil! First you promise to find me what I require, swearing to me that you will be of the greatest assistance, only to then turn your back on me and steal what I have for yourself!"

"It was not deliberately done," James answered, though Lord Kingshill's voice grew louder, his anger becoming more evident by the minute.

"Now you expect me to turn away from Lady Prudence, simply because *you* have decided that you want her more than I? And then, rather than attempt to make amends, you refuse to assist me any further! How dare you treat me in such a way?"

Seeing a few people around them begin to glance towards them, their eyes lit with curiosity, James began to back away, refusing to let any gossip come from this.

"I am sorry, my friend. Do excuse me."

"Sorry? Is that all you can say?"

"Gentlemen!"

James held both hands up as Lord Henstridge, the gentleman hosting the ball, came towards them.

"Forgive my friend, Lord Henstridge. He is a little in his cups and–"

"I am sober enough to tell you *all*," Lord Kingshill interrupted, his voice growing even louder, "that I am courting Lady Prudence!"

Fear clutched at James' heart.

"You are mistaken!" he exclaimed, as a few of the other guests now gasped in shock at what was playing out before them. "I am *betrothed* to Lady Prudence and soon intend to marry her!" This brought yet more exclamations from the crowd who all either looked to each other or looked to James, Lord Kingshill or Lord Henstridge himself. James lifted his chin, silently challenging his friend but Lord Kingshill only sneered. "*I* am betrothed to Lady Prudence," James said again, only for Lord Kingshill to slice the air with his hand.

"No, *I* am the one betrothed to her!"

The crowd around them made so much noise at this remark that James was sure even the orchestra had stopped playing to listen to the conversation.

"There is only one way for us to sort this matter out, I believe," Lord Henstridge said, slowly, looking just as confused as the other guests around him. "We must find Lady Prudence and speak with her, and *then,* we will know the truth."

"Lady Prudence?" One of the ladies near him touched James' arm and, glancing at her, he nodded. The lady then exchanged a glance with her friend, her eyes wide with obvious surprise. "Goodness, I did not think that anyone would ever pursue *that* particular young lady after what she did!"

Fire tied itself around James' heart as questions began to fill his mind about what such a thing could be, only to then remind himself of all the many things *he* had done that had burned his reputation into nothing but ashes and smoke.

"Her reputation is far better than mine, I assure you," he said, turning and speaking directly to the lady, making her blush with embarrassment. "I care deeply for the lady and will be very glad when the wedding day is set."

"When *my* wedding day is set, you mean!" Lord Kingshill cried, catching everyone's attention. "You need not try to steal my betrothed from me, just as you have stolen coin and the like before! *I* am to marry the lady and you–"

"Let us go and find the lady," James interrupted, silently praying that Lady Prudence would forgive the interruption and, thereafter, answer in the affirmative that yes, she would marry him rather than Lord Kingshill. "That way, this matter can be settled for good."

Without waiting, he turned on his heel and began to

stride across the room, his eyes searching desperately for the one lady he most wished to find. A glance over his shoulder told him that not only were Lord Kingshill and Lord Henstridge following, but so also was almost half the room! Chewing on the edge of his lip, James' heart began to beat a little more furiously as he searched for Lady Prudence. They had not discussed betrothal, only courtship, but there was no time for such things now. Would she accept him? Would she be willing to marry him? And, most of all, would she truly believe every single word of devotion and promise that he made?

CHAPTER SEVENTEEN

"*M*ama? Papa? I – I must speak with you."

Prudence sat down quickly, hoping that by clasping her hands under the table, they would not see how she trembled. After her walk around the park earlier that morning and speaking with Lord Childers, she felt overwhelmed with thoughts. Although she had managed to sneak back into the house without being seen by anyone, she had not returned to her bed. Yes, she had changed back into her night things and taken the morning chocolate brought to her by her maid but all the while, she had done nothing but think of Lord Childers. Now, the moment had come for her to speak to her parents about what he proposed.

"Yes?" Her mother smiled at her, then gestured to the teapot. "Would you like to have a cup of tea before you begin? You have not eaten a single thing thus far and you must be thirsty, at least!"

Prudence shook her head.

"I am quite all right, I assure you. Might I begin?"

Her mother tilted her head, looking at her.

"This is a serious matter, yes?"

"Yes."

"My dear."

Reaching across, Lady Lymington touched her husband's hand, causing him to look away from the newspaper he held in his hand and look instead at Prudence.

"There is something you wish to say, Prudence dear?" Lord Lymington smiled warmly. "What is it?" A faint flicker came into his eyes. "Is it that you hope now to remove your connection with Lord Kingshill? I confess that I would not find that a disappointment if you were to do so."

"My dear!"

Lady Lymington hissed but Prudence smiled, feeling a little relieved that her father had spoken so.

"It does make this conversation a little easier, to know that you feel that way, Papa," she said slowly, hearing her mother's swift intake of breath. "Yes, I should like to end my connection to Lord Kingshill before it has even begun!"

Both of her parents glanced at each other though, much to Prudence's relief, her father immediately began to smile.

"I am glad to hear it. That is not because I do not want you to be happy, but I am sure that Lord Kingshill is not at all the sort of gentleman you should be connecting yourself to."

"I quite agree," Prudence answered, though Lady Lymington looked a little sorrowful, her expression rather downcast. "However, I do not intend to become a spinster. That is not something I want for my future. Therefore, rather than stepping away from Lord Kingshill without any other possibilities laid out ahead of me, I have instead accepted an offer from another gentleman."

At this, Lady Lymington let out a huge gasp, her fingers grasping the tablecloth in obvious astonishment. Prudence swallowed and said nothing, wondering if she ought to have accepted her mother's offer of a cup of tea given that her mouth had become so dry. Her father was also evidently astonished, given the way that his eyes had rounded, though he merely cleared his throat in a rather gruff manner rather than say anything.

"You... you have received another offer?" Lady Lymington whispered, as Prudence nodded. "In place of Lord Kingshill? A *reputable* gentleman?"

Prudence winced.

"No, I would not say that." Her mother's shoulders dropped instantly. "Though he has promised that he will reform himself and, thus far, he has proven himself."

Lord Lymington's hand thumped hard on the table.

"You are speaking of the Marquess of Childers, are you not?"

A little surprised, Prudence nodded.

"I am," she said, slowly. "How did you know?"

"From your description," her father answered, rubbing one hand over his chin. "I spoke to him recently."

"You... you did?"

"I did, yes." Lord Lymington smiled. "I thanked him for keeping the announcement away from the *ton* when Lord Kingshill was in his cups. I thought it would have been a most inappropriate time, and found myself rather surprised to see that another rake, such as he, was aware of the same thing. I did not expect that he would have cared about you in such a way, but it was clear to me that he did."

"He has offered himself in place of Lord Kingshill," Prudence told him, a little flushed now. "He has said that he will speak to Lord Kingshill, and I said that I would speak to both of you. I know that he is a rake, I understand that he is a scoundrel, but he has sworn to reform himself – and thus far, these last few weeks, he *has* done that."

"Yes, he has."

"You – you cannot be seriously considering this, Lymington!"

Prudence's shoulders rounded and she dropped her head as her mother instantly began to shake her head, her distrust of the gentleman clear.

"I am considering it, yes," Lord Lymington answered, mildly. "Lord Childers is a rogue, yes, but we have just agreed to Lord Kingshill, so why would we not accept him?"

Lady Lymington blinked and then threw up her hands.

"Because he is even *more* a scoundrel than Lord Kingshill! Do you not know of his reputation?"

"He cares for me." Prudence closed her eyes the moment the words came out of her mouth, feeling her mother's gaze shooting through her. She trembled a little as she spoke, but she forced herself to speak words of truth anyway. "And I believe that I care for him." Silence met her words and, anxiety raking up her spine,

Prudence opened her eyes and looked at her mother who was staring, wide-eyed, at Prudence.

"I believe him, Mama," she continued, her voice catching. "He is a rogue, yes, but he has not done anything which would make me question his present determination to be devoted to me. The fact that he has spoken to me truthfully, confessing his initial motivations in arranging the match, and then explaining how his thinking has changed significantly since then, makes me believe that his words are genuine. I can see now that I would have nothing but misery should I marry Lord Kingshill, but with Lord Childers, do I not have a small hope of happiness?"

Lady Lymington closed her eyes and let out a long, slow breath.

"You have a small chance, yes, but there is still so much danger. I was never hopeful that you would have any sort of happiness with Lord Kingshill, but I did not know if... well..." She shook her head, her voice breaking. "I want only the best for you, my dear. I care for you so very much, and I do not want you to have a life of misery."

"I think that I have a better chance of happiness with Lord Childers than I would ever have had with Lord Kingshill."

"I would agree," Lord Lymington murmured, reaching out to take his wife's hand. "Come, my dear, consider all that your daughter is saying, and all that Lord Childers has said to her. I will say that I too was rather surprised at his consideration of her, and it did make me question whether or not there was a chance that this very thing might occur."

Hope filled Prudence's heart.

"Then you will permit him to court me? Knowing that betrothal will soon follow?"

Lord Lymington smiled and nodded.

"Yes, my dear. Of course. The choice I will give to you, but I believe that the decision has already been made, yes?"

Prudence nodded, tears beginning to threaten, her voice hoarse.

"Yes, Papa. I thank you." Her vision was a little blurred when she looked at her mother, who was now gripping her husband's hand tightly. "Mama?"

Lady Lymington took a moment and then, with a wobbly smile, nodded.

"Yes, Prudence. If you are sure, then I will not hold back my consent, even though it is not needed."

"Thank you." Prudence rose from her chair and, coming across to her mother, went to embrace her. "I think that I will be happy, Mama. Even if I am married to a rogue."

"A *reformed* rogue," Lady Lymington stated, firmly, managing to smile. "I will make certain to speak to Lord Childers myself and make sure that he is fully aware of what my expectations are of him, as your husband!"

Laughing, Prudence went to embrace her father, her heart happier than it had been in some time.

"I am sure that he will take it very well, Mama. I thank you."

"Let us hope that Lord Kingshill takes this news as

well as we have!" Lord Lymington laughed, hugging her tightly. "What an excellent end to the Season this will be!"

"Prudence?"

Prudence smiled and made to greet Miss Rockwell, only to see her friend's expression as she hurried towards her.

"Anna? What is wrong?"

"Many people are speaking of you!" her friend exclaimed, her eyes wide. "I believe that there has been an argument between Lord Kingshill and Lord Childers and now they are both coming in search of you so that you might put an end to it."

"An argument?" Prudence's heart began to beat hard. "What sort of argument?"

"I do not know, but half the *ton* are coming with them!" Miss Rockwell grasped Prudence's hand. "Has something happened? Is Lord Childers–"

"Oh!" Gasping aloud, Prudence stared back into her friend's eyes. "I am not to be betrothed to Lord Kingshill any longer. I am going to wed Lord Childers, just as you suggested."

Despite the worry in her eyes, Miss Rockwell smiled brightly.

"How wonderful! I am delighted to hear it! How did such a thing come about?"

Prudence hesitated, her eyes now searching the ballroom.

"I – I shall explain all, but mayhap I should go and find Lord Childers? I do not want to garner the attention of every single person in the *ton*."

Miss Rockwell nodded.

"I think you should. Come, I will go with you." Looping her arm through Prudence's, they walked a little further forward, out of the shadows and back into the crowd of guests. Prudence felt as though every step was heavy, her legs weighted and desperate to hold her back from the scrutiny that was going to follow. She had not been a part of the *ton* for a long time and, no doubt, some of them would know what it was she had done as regarded Lord Newling and might now begin to speak of it again. Would they tell Lord Childers of it? What would he think if they did? "There."

Miss Rockwell turned her head and nodded in the direction of a small group of people who appeared to be walking as one, following two figures. One was Lord Kingshill and the other, Lord Childers. Prudence's heart twisted and she caught her breath, trying to fight the desire to step back, to step away from the many looks, the many whispers and the many remarks which were soon to be directed towards her.

"I see them."

Swallowing her fear, Prudence lifted her chin and, with Miss Rockwell beside her, she made her way towards the gentlemen. The moment one of those within the group caught sight of her, it seemed as though a ripple ran right around the room. The whispers grew into a torrent and then a great and heavy wave that felt, to Prudence, as though it crashed over her. Her breath hitched, her chest was tight, and her hands were suddenly very cold as she continued to walk towards them.

Then, Lord Childers looked at her and, with a broad smile on his face, began to come towards her. Lord Kingshill followed, though he appeared to be a good deal more ill-tempered given the scowl which pulled at his face.

"Whatever could their argument have been about?" Miss Rockwell whispered as Prudence forced a smile to her lips. "Do you think that they argued about you?"

"I do not know," Prudence returned, as Lord Childers came close to her, bowing low. "Good evening, Lord Childers." She looked at Lord Kingshill as he came closer. "And to you also, Lord Kingshill."

Glancing around, she caught sight of the gathered crowd who were all now looking toward her. Her face grew hot, but she returned her gaze quickly to Lord Childers, who was still smiling. That expression brought her a little relief, and she took a deep breath and then lifted an eyebrow.

"Lady Prudence, as you know, you and I are courting," Lord Kingshill stated, stepping forward so that he was the nearest one to her. "I do not know why Lord Childers now believes that *he* has taken my place, but I want you now to tell both him and the other guests gathered here that it is not as he says. "

"And if you are wrong?" Lord Childers asked, his eyebrow lifting. "Then, will you step back? Will you step away without any further protestations?"

Lord Kingshill lifted his chin.

"I shall."

"Oh?"

Lord Childers' voice was filled with doubt.

"I shall!" Lord Kingshill exclaimed, speaking a little more loudly now. "If Lady Prudence states, here and now, that we are not courting, then I shall step back without further hesitation." Prudence frowned, seeing the sudden glint in Lord Kingshill's eyes. Clearly, Lord Childers had already spoken to him, so why now was he speaking with such confidence? Did he truly believe that she would agree with his statement, simply because he demanded it? They had barely spoken, and he had not given her more than a glance here and there when they *had* been in company, so what was it that he thought would pull her towards him? "We have an agreement, Lady Prudence," Lord Kingshill stated, looking down at her, his eyes sharpening. "We are to court, then we are to become betrothed and marry. You shall bear the heirs to my line, and we shall live as husband and wife. Is that not so?"

"Or is it that *we* are betrothed?"

Prudence's eyebrows lifted as Lord Childers' eyes searched her face, widening a little at the edges. No, they were not yet betrothed, she wanted to say, though it seemed that was what he had spoken to the crowd, given the way that they were murmuring. It did not matter to her, however, for though that question had not yet come from his lips, though he had not formally asked her to wed, she was not about to refuse him. Having spoken to both her mother and father and received their consent for the match, it did not matter to her one bit if they were now betrothed rather than courting! That had always been what she had hoped for, what she had intended, and this was now being offered to her, it seemed.

"I–"

"Lady Prudence," Lord Kingshill interrupted, before Prudence could continue speaking. "I should like to remind you that, though we all have something of a reputation here, there are... *reasons* for our reputation to be so. I will fully admit to being a rake and find myself a little proud of it, I admit." He snorted as he gestured to Lord Childers. "This gentleman has decided that he shall reform himself a little, though I think that in itself is foolishness, I confess."

"It is not foolishness!" Prudence exclaimed, only for Lord Kingshill to hold up one finger to her, silencing her.

"As I was saying, we each have a reputation," he said, a little more slowly and a good deal more quietly now. "I do wonder if you have told Lord Childers the reason for *your* standing as a wallflower, Lady Prudence?" Prudence blinked, a sudden fear clutching her heart. "I confess that I was a little intrigued as to why you were a wallflower, and I shall also state that Lord Childers' explanation of it was a little lacking in detail. While I was sure that you were certainly not ruined, there was still more I wanted to discover. And I *have* discovered it, though I did not think it of any benefit to share with Lord Childers at the time. Mayhap now I should?" He smiled and tilted his head as though she were a child and he simply teasing her. "It was somewhat difficult to find out the truth, I must admit. I shall suppose that you are rather glad that the *ton* does not know all of it, does not know of your manipulation and your coercion. And Lord

Childers certainly does not know of it either, else he would not have described you in such sweet terms to me!"

Miss Rockwell grasped Prudence's hand.

"Do not listen to him," she hissed, though Prudence could not take her eyes from Lord Kingshill's face, such was her fear.

She could see exactly what he was threatening, could see all that he was laying out for her. There were two paths before her now. One where she said nothing, agreed to wed Lord Kingshill, and took her place by his side – lonely, broken, and unloved. Or she could take the other path, where the truth would be revealed, the *ton* would know all, and Lord Childers might easily reject her. Then she would be left just as alone as she had been at the beginning, but without any hope of ever making a match again.

"Do not listen to a word Lord Kingshill says, I beg of you." Lord Childers came closer to her, his hand outstretched. "I do not care what such a thing might be. I have done far worse, I am sure!"

"Ah, but can you manage the *ton*'s rejection of you? Of you *both*?" Lord Kingshill laughed, tilting his head, bird-like. "You will have that stain lingering on your children! You will have them–"

"Please!" Prudence's voice was trembling, her whole body shaking as she squeezed Miss Rockwell's hand. Every eye was on her, making her feel as though every guest at the ball was looking at her, listening to whatever it was that she was going to say. Her heart clamoring, she looked at Miss Rockwell, feeling sweat trickle down her back. "I do not know what to do."

"Do *not* listen to Lord Kingshill!"

"But Lord Childers might turn away from me," Prudence whispered, tears in her eyes. "When he knows the truth, then–"

"Can you trust him?"

Prudence took in a long breath, barely able to form the words.

"I do not know if I can. We are so little acquainted and, though my heart has begun to form an attachment, there is still so much more that he needs to prove."

Miss Rockwell's eyes searched hers.

"Would he say the same of you, do you think? Do you believe that he too would wonder whether or not he could trust you?"

Closing her eyes, Prudence steadied herself.

"I have not told him the truth about my past but yes, I would hope that he could trust me."

"And that is what he hopes for you at this moment," Miss Rockwell stated, firmly. "I believe that you should not resign yourself to a life without love and care, Prudence. Take the risk. Even if society should turn its back on you, even if it should say that you are unworthy to be in its presence, you will still have Lord Childers." She pressed Prudence's hand and smiled. "And you shall have me."

Prudence blinked away her tears, her stomach coiling with fear.

"But you do not know what I have done."

"I do not need to know. I know who you are *now* and

that is all that matters." Miss Rockwell looked at Lord Childers. "And that is all that matters when it comes to Lord Childers too."

Understanding what her friend was saying, Prudence hesitated and then looked back to the two gentlemen. Lord Kingshill was standing tall and proud, his lips curved into a cruel smirk as though he knew all too well that what he had said had taken root. Evidently, he believed that his threats would be enough for her to give in to him, expecting her to reject Lord Childers and bend to his will. Lord Childers, on the other hand, was gazing at her with what looked like desperation in his eyes. He was chewing on the edge of his lip, his hands curled into fists and one foot tapping lightly on the floor. He did not have the same confidence as Lord Kingshill exuded and certainly had no bravado about him. Could she really trust that no matter what Lord Kingshill told him, he would still continue in his connection with her? Would they still marry? Would he still feel the same way about her?

"We are all waiting, Lady Prudence," Lord Kingshill said, his voice light and mirthful as though this was all something to be laughed at, something that the *ton* would find mirthful. "Tell us all the truth, will you not?"

"The truth." Taking her hand from Miss Rockwell's, Prudence took a step forward and then, lifting her chin a notch, looked directly into Lord Kingshill's eyes. "Here is the truth."

An idea came to her as she spoke and, with a slight lift of one side of her mouth, she began. Whether it would be of any benefit to her, she did not know, but it was her only hope. Perhaps telling the *ton* the truth about Lord Kingshill – even though he was a rogue – would be enough to have them push back from him all the more.

"Lady Prudence, please," Lord Childers began, though his hands then fell back to his sides when she looked to him, his shoulders rounding as though he knew exactly what it was that she was going to say.

"Here is the truth," Prudence began, speaking loudly enough for almost everyone to hear. "Lord Kingshill *did* suggest that we court, with the expectation that betrothal and matrimony would follow. What he did not initially state, however, was that he did such a thing solely so that the heir to his title would follow. He made it quite clear that he did not care a jot for me, stating that *I* had to speak with my father about the arrangement rather than Lord Kingshill going to speak with him, himself. That is how little a gentleman he is." A few murmurs began to move around the room and, filled with a little more confidence, Prudence took a deep breath, noting how Lord Kingshill's sneer had begun to fade away. "My father was reluctant, but I was assured that Lord Kingshill would attempt to reform himself, that he would do all that he could to be an upstanding husband and reformed rogue. I did not expect love and affection, but I certainly hoped for a respectful, considerate husband, and it was with that expectation that the arrangement was made. However," she continued, her voice a little stronger now that she could see the reaction amongst the other guests, "I learned from Lord Childers – who came to speak to me out of consideration for me – that this was not as Lord Kingshill truly intended. Instead, he thought only to marry me so that the heir could be produced and, in the interim, he planned to continue in his roguish ways here in society, doing just as he pleased. He had no interest in me, expecting me to live in my own quarters of the house while he remained in his... or spent the majority of his time at the houses of others!" This statement brought a loud gasp, for even though Lord Kingshill was known to be a scoundrel, to hear of his intentions was shocking indeed. "With that revealed, Lord Childers then stated that *he* would take the place of Lord Kingshill so that I would not be without a husband, and without hope. I accepted his offer, seeing that Lord Kingshill would never be able to provide even the smallest amount of care for me, and dreading to think what sort of life I would have... and what sort of father any children we had would be given also."

Another murmur ran around the assembled group, with both gentlemen and ladies nodding in under-standing.

"Uhhh...."

Lord Kingshill made a strangled sound, which Prudence ignored.

"Even now, you see that he threatens and seeks to coerce the lady to get what he wants," Miss Rockwell cried, coming to stand beside Prudence again. "His words cannot be trusted! Nothing he says can be believed! He expects to gain whatever he desires and when he is in danger of being denied it, he threatens instead. Is that the sort of gentleman that any young lady ought to marry? Would any of you who are fathers or mothers be glad to offer up the hand of your daughter to such a fellow?" She stood beside Prudence, clearly aware of the reason behind all that Prudence had said and adding her weighty words to it. "You cannot hold anything against Lady Prudence for stepping away from Lord Kingshill, and you *certainly* cannot believe anything that Lord Kingshill says about her, not when you know the sort of gentleman he is and what he will do to get his way."

Prudence, filled with a fresh confidence, threw out one hand towards Lord Childers.

"I am betrothed to *this* gentleman!" she declared, ignoring the narrowing of Lord Kingshill's eyes, and the way that he took a step towards her, as though he wanted to silence her before she had even begun. "I am to marry Lord Childers, and I shall never be coerced into betrothing myself to the selfish, arrogant, cruel person of Lord Kingshill."

With that, she made her way directly towards Lord Childers who, taking her hand, set it on his arm and, without so much as glancing towards Lord Kingshill or anyone else, led her directly away from them all.

CHAPTER EIGHTEEN

"Thank you," James murmured, having no other thought of what to say. He found himself rather overwhelmed by what he had just witnessed and now, realizing that he was walking with his betrothed on his arm filled him with nothing but wonder. He had seen the fear in Lady Prudence's eyes and had been afraid that she would turn to Lord Kingshill again rather than lingering beside him as she had promised. Even now, he did not understand the threat that Lord Kingshill had held over her, but he was aware of it, nonetheless. The way that she had jerked back just a little when Lord Kingshill had spoken of her past, of their reputations, had told him there was some sort of weight still lingering on her shoulders, something yet unspoken, and certainly not shared with him. There was no time to speak of it now, however, for James' only thought was to find Lord and Lady Lymington.

"You can trust me, Lady Prudence," he murmured, glancing across at her as they walked together around the ballroom. "No matter what is said or what takes place, you can be certain of my commitment to you. I assure you that there is nothing that can take me from you. I feel like the gentleman who has won a great prize, a prize that I am entirely unworthy of. When you said, in front of the rest of the society, that you would marry me rather than Lord Kingshill, my heart flung itself so far up in exultation as to reach the very heights of the sky."

Lady Prudence looked back at him, her face a little pale.

"I am relieved that you were still willing to accept me," she said, softly. "There is much that I need to explain, things that I should have said to you before now." Her lips twisted for a moment. "Mayhap you will not be so willing to accept me then."

James stopped immediately, turning so that he could look straight down into Lady Prudence's face.

"I can assure you, Lady Prudence, that no matter what it is that is revealed to me, no matter what it is that is said, I shall never turn away from you." The lady said nothing for some moments, gazing back into his face as though she desperately hoped that he meant what he said. "I am a scoundrel, remember," he told her, a slight tone of irony in his voice. "There is nothing which you can have done that I cannot match, and likely a good deal worse. You have accepted me, you have given me your trust, and I can promise you that such a thing will not be thrown back at you. Instead, I will not only respect it, but value it, holding it close to my heart and reminding myself of just how fortunate I am to have you beside me." He pressed her hand. "Can you trust me in that?"

Lady Prudence took a deep breath, closed her eyes for a moment, and then nodded.

"I think that I can."

"Good." Glancing behind him, James saw the other guests still following them, gathering more and more as they went. The whispers and the gossip would soon begin, and he did not want Lady Prudence to endure anything like that. "Come now, let me get you back to your mother."

Lady Prudence fell back into step with him quickly enough, her mouth still pinched, however, as though she feared that a great disaster was going to befall them once she told him the truth. Resisting the urge to ask her what it was, so that they might discuss it and thereafter, set it aside, James let out a slow breath of relief as he came into sight of Lord and Lady Lymington.

"Good evening to you both." He bowed and then looked at Lady Prudence. "I have been told by your daughter that we have an understanding?"

Lord Lymington nodded.

"Yes, we do."

"Which is just as well, as I have had to take the circumstances and push them a little further ahead," James continued, looking over his shoulder again. "I am sure that Lady Prudence can explain to you a little more but there are already a great many of the guests come in search of her, eager to question her a little."

"Question?" Lady Lymington's eyebrows shot up but, thankfully, Lady Prudence was the one to respond. "It is not something that you need to be concerned with,

Mama. Lord Kingshill did not take his rejection particularly well and I was forced to speak publicly."

"Goodness!" Lady Lymington looked behind James and, after a moment, caught her breath. "Then we should take our leave, I think!"

James nodded and released Lady Prudence's arm.

"I think that might be best. The crowd is already growing, and they will soon want to speak to Lady Prudence again, given that we have now declared ourselves to be betrothed."

There was a breath of silence for a moment as Lady Lymington's gaze went first to her daughter and then, moved to James. He did not explain himself, did not see the need to do so, but instead, simply held the lady's gaze and nodded as though this was all the explanation she needed.

"I am sure that Prudence can explain on the way home, my dear." Lord Lymington put out one hand to his wife, urging her towards the door. "And you, Lord Childers, might you call upon me tomorrow?"

James nodded.

"Of course."

Immediately, his stomach began to twist, his heart pounding as he feared what it was that Lord Lymington would say to him about what he had done but there was no time for questions or the like. Instead, Lord Lymington turned and led his daughter away, leaving James to stand alone, wondering just how tomorrow's conversation would go... and just how much he would be able to explain.

~

Pacing up and down the hallway, James tried not to let his worries take hold of him. Last evening had been one of the most extraordinary evenings of his life, though he had not spoken a word to Lady Prudence since then. He had thought that they might have exchanged a note or two this morning, but he had not found anything to write and though the desire had been there, he had struggled to put pen to paper. Just what had she told her parents? Had she explained to them all that she had done, and all that Lord Kingshill had said? No doubt Lord Lymington would find himself angry with Lord Kingshill's threats, but the deed was done. Whether Lord Kingshill would do as he had threatened, James did not know, but he prayed that he would not.

"I thank you."

James turned, just as another gentleman stepped out into the hallway, one whom James did not recognize. He stepped aside and let the fellow pass, only for Lord Lymington to greet him.

"Thank you for being so prompt in your arrival, good sir. Forgive me for being a little tardy. There is much to do now that my daughter is betrothed!"

James put one hand to his heart and bowed.

"I thank you for permitting me to call on you – and for betrothing myself to your daughter without first speaking to you, I can only apologize."

"It is quite understandable, given what has taken place," came the reply. "Now, let us not stand together here in the hallway and converse! Please, come in."

Feeling a little less concerned, now that Lord Lymington had spoken with consideration and understanding, James did as he was asked and followed the gentleman. The study was just as he might have expected, with a large wooden desk to one side, sitting in front of some bookshelves. Lord Lymington did not go to sit down at his desk, however, but instead, gestured for James to sit down in one of two overstuffed chairs to the other side of the room. James did so quickly, rather surprised when Lord Lymington offered him a glass of brandy. If the gentleman had brought him here to berate him, to rail at him for what had happened, then surely he would not be as generous as this!

"To your wedding!" Lord Lymington smiled, holding up his glass as James blinked in surprise before finally lifting his own to his lips. "Goodness, Lord Childers, I confess that I am rather surprised to see you so astonished. What sort of reception did you think that you would receive from me today?"

"In truth, Lord Lymington, I thought that you would likely show nothing but anger," James admitted, seeing the gentleman smile. "I thought that you would be greatly upset that I had betrothed myself to Lady Prudence without even speaking to you first! I am a gentleman with a dreadful reputation – though I will admit that this is not something which ever troubled me before meeting your daughter – and to have one's daughter betrothed to someone such as I cannot be pleasing."

"It is certainly not what I had hoped for her, yes," Lord Lymington admitted, "but my dear fellow, it is better than her being wed to Lord Kingshill! You know as well as I that Lord Kingshill had no interest in Prudence and would have made her nothing more than miserable for the rest of her days. With you, however, I can see that there is a hope that she *will* be happy and contented." Tilting his head, he looked at James steadily. "You care for her, I think."

A little embarrassed, James nodded but looked away.

"I do, Lord Lymington, though I am well aware that I do not deserve to have such a young lady as she on my arm. After all that I have done, and the disrespect that I have shown to so many, I do not think for a moment that I deserve to have your consent to my marrying Lady Prudence – nor hers either!"

"But you have it," Lord Lymington said, quietly, his eyes suddenly grave. "I must ask you, however, to consider this matter with great seriousness, Lord Childers. She is my daughter, and I love her as any father loves his child. That does mean that I am concerned for her welfare, that I want what is best for her, so that I can see her happy and contented. I am entrusting her to you, Lord Childers, and that is a great responsibility. I do not think that Lord Kingshill would have taken that with any sort of seriousness, but I must hope that *you* will."

James quickly nodded.

"I do, and I will," he promised, fervency in every word that he spoke as he moved to sit a little further forward in his chair. "Lord Lymington, I did not ever expect to care for any young lady in the way that I care for Lady Prudence. I thought that, when it came time for me to wed, I would do so reluctantly and unwillingly – and yet now, here I am finding myself utterly delighted at the prospect! I want to hasten the day that will bring Lady Prudence to me as my wife, and I swear to you, as I will swear to her, that I will take my responsibility as her husband with all seriousness. I will commit myself to her happiness, I will devote myself to her care. I will not turn my back on her, I will not turn again to the ways which have been so familiar to me and yet so hurtful to so many. I can assure you of that."

It took a moment but, eventually, Lord Lymington smiled.

"That is excellent to hear," he said, a small smile drifting across his face. "I believe, for the first time since we came to London, that my daughter has a real chance of happiness... and it seems that she shall have it with the worst rogue in all of London!"

James found himself laughing along with Lord Lymington though it came more from relief than genuine good humor. He had nothing to worry himself about, it seemed, for Lord Lymington was quite contented to see his daughter wed to James. The way that it had come about had been surprising indeed, but James was, as he had said, truly grateful to now find himself attached to Lady Prudence. She was so very wonderful, gracious, considerate, and kind, and his heart was slowly filling with an increased affection for her.

All he had to do now was tell her that.

CHAPTER NINETEEN

"I do not think that I can do this."

"Of course you can." Lady Lymington smiled and urged her gently forward, one hand to the small of her back. "He is your betrothed now. You must be seen in public."

"But... but they have all been whispering about me," Prudence answered, her voice trembling. "Mama, I am sure that Lord Childers must know of it by now."

"And if he does, then all is well for you are *going* to wed regardless. He has assured you of that, has he not?"

Prudence nodded but still stayed back by the carriage, aware that Lord Childers was now looking towards her but finding it too difficult to take even the smallest step towards him.

"What will he think of me?"

"My dear." With a sigh, Lady Lymington turned around to face her, grasping both of Prudence's hands in hers. "Listen to me. The time for fear and upset is over. You have found yourself a match and though he is not the most excellent of gentlemen, he is a gentleman with a high title, with a good fortune, and with a promise that he shall reform himself. Do you think that you can consider that, rather than being fearful about your past?" Prudence swallowed tightly. "And I shall also remind you that he is a rogue," her mother added, perhaps seeing that Prudence was still reluctant. "Or certainly *was* a rogue! He has promised to reform himself, and I do believe that you can trust him in that, given what he has proven so far by his behavior. Yes, what you did was foolish and did bring you some consequences, but I am quite certain that it will not be severe enough for a rogue like him to not be able to forgive! And I am quite happy to remind him about such a thing, should there be any sort of concern." Prudence laughed at this, feeling some of her tension fade. Perhaps her mother was right. Perhaps she *could* bring herself to trust Lord Childers and, even as she told him about her past, believe that it would not be severe enough for him to step away from her. "Go, now. He is waiting for you."

Swallowing hard, Prudence began to move forward, her chest tight as she saw him smile. There was a kindness in his eyes that reached out to her heart, a tenderness warming his expression which pulled away even more of her worry.

"I am glad that you came to me," he said, as she reached him. "I was afraid that you would stay by the carriage, and I would be without you for my walk through the park!"

Prudence flushed.

"I am sorry, I–"

"I am only teasing." Lord Childers gave her a wry smile. "Perhaps I ought not to have said such a thing. I can understand your concern, my dear lady. The *ton* can be a monstrous beast, can it not? And this is our first time walking together since the news of our betrothal was made known."

"Which was only two days ago, and yet I have heard that the gossip and the rumors have already been rushing around London." Prudence squeezed her eyes closed for a moment. "My friend, Miss Rockwell, told me of it. Not so that I would feel terribly bad or afraid, however, simply so that I was aware of it."

He smiled.

"I understand. Though we can ignore all that is said now, I am sure."

"Even what Lord Kingshill has been saying?"

Prudence watched Lord Childers as she spoke, waiting to see if there was a flicker of understanding in his eyes, something there that told her that he understood exactly what she was talking about.

There was nothing.

"I do not know if Lord Kingshill has said a word as yet," Lord Childers told her, offering her his arm. "Shall we walk, Lady Prudence?" She took it and nodded, finding her mouth going dry as she fought to find the words to tell him all about what she had done. They would not come, however, her fears grew bigger and bigger with every step they took. "I should like to make it very clear that you do not *have* to tell me anything," Lord Childers said, softly. "If it is troubling you so severely, then I will not require you to tell me anything."

Prudence's heart leaped.

"You do not want to know?"

"It is not that I have no interest, for to say otherwise would be a lie," Lord Childers answered, still speaking in a very gentle manner, "but only to say that if it would bring you more distress and upset, then I would be contented for you *not* to tell me of it. I will not turn away from you whether I know of it or not."

The kindness and the trust he showed her were so great that Prudence felt like weeping. She wanted to hold her secret tight to her chest, wanted to pretend that she had nothing to tell him and thus, keep her past and all that she had done solely to herself, but her conscience would not let her. Here was this gentleman, generous enough in his consideration of her to let her keep all she wished to herself, offering her such a great amount of trust that she had no other choice but to respond in kind.

"I believe that you will not step away from me, even if I tell you this," she said, breathlessly, as Lord Childers nodded. "I do not want to have anything between us. I do not want to have any secrets and nor do I want to have you hear any rumors which have no real truth to them. Therefore, I will tell you the true reason behind my standing as a wallflower."

"Thank you."

Glancing around her for fear that there would be others who overheard her, Prudence took another breath – and then another, for her fears began to cling tightly to her heart, telling her not to say anything to him, demanding that she keep her secret.

She spoke anyway.

"I was determined to marry well," she began, her voice shaking as she fought to even so much as glance at him. "I am the daughter of an Earl and, therefore, I thought that I should marry a rank above myself. I wanted to marry a Marquess or even a Duke." Heat climbed up into her cheeks. "It may have been foolish and mayhap I ought to have simply considered my happiness rather than my standing, but that was where my determination lay."

"I am sure that many a young lady would think the same thing," Lord Childers said, shrugging lightly. "You cannot be the only young lady with such a desire."

"Indeed, but they would not all have done as I did." Closing her eyes for a moment, Prudence attempted to bolster her courage. "Lord Childers, I did something so unspeakably wrong, society should have turned its back on me completely. It is only by sheer good fortune that the *ton* did not know of it in its entirety, though some certainly did."

Lord Childers reached out his free hand and settled it on hers for just a moment.

"Remember, you do not need to tell me."

"But I *want* to," Prudence murmured, her stomach twisting as she kept her gaze away from him still. "I do not want there to be any secrets between us." With another breath, she set her shoulders and let her free hand curl tightly into a fist. "I found a gentleman who I thought I should like to marry. He was a Marquess, well-mannered, and with a good fortune, but though I tried to catch his attention, I quickly realized that there were too many young ladies within the *ton* who were doing the same thing as I. Thus," she continued, her heart pounding and filling her veins with a twisting anxiety, "I determined that I should force a match between us, by having society find us in a somewhat... compromising position."

Lord Childers turned his head towards her sharply and Prudence dropped hers so that she could not even see him out of the corner of her eye.

"I see."

He said nothing more and Prudence, daring to glance at him, saw him frown.

"I did not succeed, of course," she finished, wanting to have her confession completed just as soon as she could. "The gentleman was unaware of my intentions and did not know at all what had happened."

"How could that be?"

Wincing, Prudence turned her head away entirely, her fingers curling tightly.

"I – I purchased something which I placed within his brandy glass," she whispered, wondering if he could hear her. "I was able to lead him to a quiet room without his awareness and then I waited in the hope of being discovered. And, what is worse," she added, knowing that this was the last thing for her to say, "I attempted to do so on more than one occasion. And none of my attempts succeeded. However, the *ton* were aware that I had done *something* on that first occasion, and thus I became a wallflower."

"And you thought that, if you forced this match, then you would be able to regain your position," Lord Childers said slowly, as Prudence nodded, still unable to look at him. "Might I ask if you had any particular feelings for the gentleman?"

"No, none!" Prudence exclaimed, her eyes finding his in an instant. "It was not about emotion. It was *never* about what I felt or what he felt for me. Instead, all that I thought about was my social standing and my require-ment for a suitable match."

Lord Childers let out a breath and then shook his head, his eyes now turned to the path rather than to her.

"Well, out of all that I had thought you might say, that was not something I had anticipated!"

Shame burned into Prudence's heart.

"But if I were to tell you all of my past wrongdoings, then I can assure you, you would feel as though you were nothing but an angel," he continued, turning his head towards her as a smile pulled at his lips. "Thank you for telling me, Lady Prudence. I am grateful to know of it."

She blinked at him.

"That... that is all that you are going to say?"

Lord Childers' eyebrows lifted.

"Is there something else that you should *like* me to say to you?"

Utterly astonished, Prudence stared at him for a long moment, no longer walking but simply standing by his side, gazing up into his face and seeing that it was just as he said. He had no anger, no upset, and certainly nothing that would express any sort of discontent. Rather, there was a hint of a smile at the edge of his lips and a softness about his eyes which she had never once expected to see.

"I – I do not understand," she whispered, tears of gratitude in her eyes. "I was sure that you would turn away from me, that even though you might be true to your word and marry me still, you would look at me in a very different light."

Lord Childers shrugged his shoulders again.

"It is not as severe as you might think, Lady Prudence. It is not as though I can dare to hold anything against you either, given my past!" Smiling down into her eyes, he took in a long breath and then lifted her hand to press it to his lips. A gentle kiss settled there, and Prudence's heart warmed, her whole body free now of the worry and the anxiety that had tied itself around her for the last few days.

"There now," he murmured, tilting his head to look at her. "It is all out in open now, is it not? There is nothing that you need to worry about any longer. We will marry, we will live at my estate, and I shall give you all of my time, attention, and devotion, proving to you that I truly am a reformed rogue."

"I already am convinced of that," she breathed, wishing desperately that her mother was not nearby and that they were somewhere alone simply so that she might throw herself into his arms. "I trust you, Lord Childers, truly. My heart is overwhelmed by all that you have offered me, by all that you have *given* me, and I cannot help but be grateful for it."

"As I am grateful for you!" he exclaimed, stepping a little closer. "The only reason I have changed, the only reason I have turned from my previous ways is because of you. You have captured me, Prudence. You have captured me *utterly* and I cannot imagine being without you by my side."

"But what if Lord Kingshill speaks of this to every-one? What if the *ton* believe him?"

Lord Childers smiled.

"What should that matter to us? We are contented, are we not? We will find happiness and joy at our estate and, in time, whatever Lord Kingshill chooses to say will be forgotten. Though," he continued, a grin creeping up one side of his mouth, "I do believe that after all that you said, the *ton* will be all the less likely to listen to him! You did well there, Prudence."

"I thank you."

With a nod, Lord Childers turned, and they began to walk again, though Prudence let out a long, contented sigh of relief as she did so. The air smelled sweeter, the sky seemed lighter, and the sun even warmer than before, and all because she had told Lord Childers everything. He had accepted her regardless, had not held anything against her, and now, all there was in her future was hope and happiness. She could barely take it in.

"Oh!" She stopped dead, turning to look at Lord Childers, her eyes wide. "There is something else I forgot to tell you about."

Lord Childers blew out a breath and ran one hand over his forehead.

"Really? What can it be?"

Blushing, Prudence waved one hand vaguely.

"It is nothing overly serious, I suppose. It is only to say that the gentleman I thought to capture, the one that I thought to marry? He is now wed to my sister." At this, Lord Childers mouth fell open, and Prudence could not help but laugh. After a moment, he began to laugh with her, though there was evident relief in his expression as he did so. "There is nothing more, I assure you!" she cried, as she slipped her hand through his arm so they might walk arm in arm for a time. "That is all that I have to say."

"I will not pretend that I am not both surprised and relieved!" Lord Childers chuckled, leaning into her just a little as they walked together again. "But if you are sure that you did not ever have a small amount of feeling for him, then—"

"I have never once felt anything for Lord Newling, I assure you," Prudence interrupted, her heart quickening suddenly as she looked up into his eyes again. "The only gentleman that I have ever considered in such a way, the only one who has ever affected my heart in that particular manner is... well, it is you, Lord Childers."

The smile that spread across his face now shone light into his eyes and made Prudence's heart sing with happiness.

"You have brought about the same feelings within my own heart, Prudence," he told her, softly. "And I am certain that, by the time we marry, it shall overflow with both affection and love."

EPILOGUE

"*A*nd so, we are wed!"

"Yes, we are." Prudence, hand in hand with Lord Childers, meandered along the path towards her father's estate. The wedding ceremony had just taken place and her nervousness, though significant, had not taken away a single moment of joy from the service. Her mother, father, sister, and brother-in-law had all been present, as had Miss Rockwell and *her* betrothed, as well as Lord and Lady Drakewater. There had been a few friends and more relatives, but the only person Prudence had cared about had been Lord Childers. In the weeks between their betrothal and their wedding day, she had felt her affection grow all the more steadily, to the point that she had woken in the morning thinking about him and had retired with her mind full of wishes and hopes.

"I do hope that your father does not mind that we sent the carriage ahead of us so that we might walk back to the estate," Lord Childers murmured, his eyes dazzling her with their intensity. "The wedding breakfast will be waiting for us."

"Then let it wait," Prudence answered, finding her steps slowing as she gazed back into her husband's eyes. Lord Childers stopped completely and, after a moment, turned to face her. Then, very gently as though he had never done such a thing before, he wrapped his arms carefully around her and pulled her a little closer to him.

All of her breath left her body as Prudence looked up at him, her heart clamoring with anticipation. They had never stood as close to each other as this before and though she had found her desire for his kiss growing, she had never dared reach for it. He had not offered it either, perhaps afraid that what she knew of his roguish ways would color her perception of it and yet, Prudence had caught the lingering glances he had sent her and had dared to hope that he craved that moment just as much as she did.

"You are Lady Childers now," he said softly, reaching up one hand to brush a curl away from her cheek, tucking it lightly behind her ear. "You are my wife."

"I am." Her skin prickled, heated from where his fingers had brushed against it. "And you are my husband."

"Your *devoted* husband," he reminded her, his smile soft. "I will not let you forget that, Prudence, for I am determined to make it plain to you every single day."

She smiled and then, licking her lips, let her hands reach up to settle against his shoulders.

"You have already proven yourself in your devotion to me, Childers," she answered, seeing how his eyes flared as she slipped her hands about his neck. "I must confess something more to you, however."

"Oh?" Surprise leapt into his eyes though he did not move an inch from her. "What is it?"

She smiled then, her anticipation growing.

"I confess to you that my heart no longer holds an affection for you." Seeing him frown, she hurried her words, wanting him to understand rather than be injured. "Instead, it holds love."

Lord Childers' mouth dropped open, his eyes rounding and for some moments, he simply stared at her. Prudence merely smiled, wanting him to be convinced of it, only for him to let out a long hiss of breath, shaking his head as he did so.

"I do not deserve your affection nor your love, Prudence." His voice was low and a little hoarse. "You honor me with such a thing."

"You need not speak so," she answered, her fingers now twining through his hair, a little astonished at her own boldness. "We have found each other, have we not? Despite our past foolishness, despite our past. That is something to be wondered at, something to be delighted in."

Lord Childers considered and then, after another moment, smiled at her.

"I suppose that is quite true," he agreed, his head beginning to lower. "Though I do not think that I shall ever stop being grateful for you. You have brought me so much joy, so much happiness, that I cannot help but love you. I have wanted to tell you that for these last few weeks, but I have held those words back, waiting for the right time to confess it."

Prudence smiled up at him, her eyes blinking back tears of joy.

"I think that you have chosen the right moment."

With a small smile, Lord Childers dropped his head and kissed her lightly. It was not a long, heavy kiss but only the very gentlest of kisses, one which left her both satisfied and longing for more. With a sigh, she leaned into him all the more, but Lord Childers broke it, lifting his hands so that he might frame her face.

"I love you, Prudence," he said, a good deal more firmly now. "I do not want you to ever doubt it."

She pulled her hands from his neck and set one against his heart.

"I know that your heart beats for me," she whispered, "just as mine beats for you. I love you, Lord Childers and I believe I always shall."

With a smile, he lowered his head to kiss her again.

"Just as I love you," he murmured against her lips, before pulling her close to him again.

A HARROWING JOURNEY FOR PRUDENCE! I am glad she found her happy ever after!

Did you miss the first book in the series? The Wallflower's Unseen Charm Read ahead for a sneak peek!

Do you love boxsets? Check out my upcoming release Only for Love Boxset

MY DEAR READER

Thank you for reading and supporting my books! I hope this story brought you some escape from the real world into the always captivating Regency world. A good story, especially one with a happy ending, just brightens your day and makes you feel good! If you enjoyed the book, would you leave a review on Amazon? Reviews are always appreciated.

Below is a complete list of all my books! Why not click and see if one of them can keep you entertained for a few hours?

The Duke's Daughters Series
The Duke's Daughters: A Sweet Regency Romance
Boxset
A Rogue for a Lady
My Restless Earl
Rescued by an Earl
In the Arms of an Earl
The Reluctant Marquess (Prequel)

A Smithfield Market Regency Romance
The Smithfield Market Romances: A Sweet Regency
Romance Boxset
The Rogue's Flower

Saved by the Scoundrel
Mending the Duke
The Baron's Malady

The Returned Lords of Grosvenor Square
The Returned Lords of Grosvenor Square: A Regency
Romance Boxset
The Waiting Bride
The Long Return
The Duke's Saving Grace
A New Home for the Duke

The Spinsters Guild
The Spinsters Guild: A Sweet Regency Romance Boxset
A New Beginning
The Disgraced Bride
A Gentleman's Revenge
A Foolish Wager
A Lord Undone

Convenient Arrangements
Convenient Arrangements: A Regency Romance
Collection
A Broken Betrothal
In Search of Love
Wed in Disgrace
Betrayal and Lies
A Past to Forget
Engaged to a Friend

Landon House

Landon House: A Regency Romance Boxset
Mistaken for a Rake
A Selfish Heart
A Love Unbroken
A Christmas Match
A Most Suitable Bride
An Expectation of Love

Second Chance Regency Romance
Second Chance Regency Romance Boxset
Loving the Scarred Soldier
Second Chance for Love
A Family of her Own
A Spinster No More

Soldiers and Sweethearts
Soldiers and Sweethearts Boxset
To Trust a Viscount
Whispers of the Heart
Dare to Love a Marquess
Healing the Earl
A Lady's Brave Heart

Ladies on their Own: Governesses and Companions
Ladies on their Own Boxset
More Than a Companion
The Hidden Governess
The Companion and the Earl
More than a Governess
Protected by the Companion

A Family for Christmas
Mistletoe Magic: A Regency Romance
Heart, Homes & Holidays: A Sweet Romance Anthology

Christmas Kisses Series
Christmas Kisses Box Set
The Lady's Christmas Kiss
The Viscount's Christmas Queen
Her Christmas Duke

Happy Reading!
All my love,
Rose

A SNEAK PEEK OF THE WALLFLOWER'S UNSEEN CHARM

PROLOGUE

"*Y*ou must promise me that you will *try*."

Miss Joy Bosworth rolled her eyes at her mother.

"Try to be more like my elder sisters, yes? That *is* what you mean, is it not?"

"And what is wrong with being like them?" Lady Halifax's stern tone told Joy in no uncertain terms that to criticize Bettina, Sarah, and Mary – all three of whom had married within the last few years – was a very poor decision indeed. Wincing, Joy fell silent and dropped her gaze to her lap as her beleaguered lady's maid continued to fix her hair. This was the third time that her lady's maid had set her hair, for the first two attempts had been deemed entirely unsuitable by Joy's mother – though quite what was wrong with it, Joy had been completely unable to see.

"You are much too forward, too quick to give your opinion," her mother continued, gazing at Joy's reflection in the looking glass, her eyes narrowing a little. "All of your elder sisters are quiet, though Bettina perhaps a little too much so, but their husbands greatly appreciate that about them! They speak when they are asked to speak, give their opinion when it is desired and otherwise say very little when it comes to matters which do not concern them. *You,* on the other hand, speak when you are *not* asked to do so, give your opinion most readily, and say a great deal on *any* subject even when it does not concern you!"

Hearing the strong emphasis, Joy chose not to drop her head further, as her mother might have expected, but instead to lift her chin and look back steadily. She was not about to be cowed when it came to such a trait. In some ways, she was rather proud of her determination to speak as she thought, for she was the only one of her sisters who did so. Mayhap it was simply because she was the youngest, but Joy did not truly know why - she had always been determined to speak up for herself and, simply because she was in London, was not, she thought, cause to alter herself now!

"You must find a suitable husband!" Exclaiming aloud, Lady Halifax threw up her hands, perhaps seeing the glint of steel in Joy's eyes. "Continuing to behave as you are will not attract anyone to you, I can assure you of that!"

"The *right* gentleman would still be attracted," Joy shot back, adding her own emphasis. "There must be some amongst society who do not feel the same way as you, Mother. I do not seek to disagree with you, only to suggest that there might be a little more consideration in some, or even a different viewpoint altogether!"

"I know what I am talking about!" Lady Halifax smote Joy gently on the shoulder though her expression was one of frustration. "I have already had three daughters wed and it would do you well to listen to me and my advice."

Joy did not know what to say. Yes, she had listened to her mother on many an occasion, but that did not mean that she had to take everything her mother said to heart... and on this occasion, she was certain that Lady Halifax was quite wrong.

"If I am not true to who I am, Mama, then will that not make for a very difficult marriage?"

"A difficult marriage?" This was said with such a degree of astonishment that Joy could not help but smile. "There is no such thing as a difficult marriage, not unless one of the two parties *within* the marriage itself attempts to make it so. Do you not understand, Joy? I am telling you to alter yourself so that you do *not* cause any difficulties, both for yourself now, and for your husband in the future."

The smile on Joy's face slipped and then blew away, her forehead furrowing as she looked at her mother again. Lady Halifax was everything a lady of quality ought to be, and she had trained each of her daughters to be as she was... except that Joy had never been the success her other daughters had been. Even now, the thought of stepping into marriage with a gentleman she barely knew, simply because he was deemed suitable, was rather horrifying to Joy, and was made all the worse by the idea that she would somehow have to pretend to be someone she was not!

"As I have said, Joy, you will try."

This time, Joy realized, it was not a question her mother had been asking her but a statement. A statement which said that she was expected to do nothing other than what her mother said – and to do so without question also.

I shall not lie.

"I think my hair is quite presentable now, Mama." Steadfastly refusing to either agree with or refuse what her mother had said, Joy sat up straight in her chair, her head lifting, her shoulders dropping low as she turned her head from side to side. "Very elegant, I must say."

"The ribbon is not the right color."

Joy resisted the urge to roll her eyes for what would be the second time.

"Mama, it is a light shade of green and it is threaded through the many braids Clara has tied my hair into. It is quite perfect and cannot be faulted. Besides, it does match the gown perfectly. You made certain of that yourself."

So saying, she threw a quick smile to her lady's maid and saw a twitch of Clara's lips before the maid bowed her head, stepping back so that Lady Halifax would not see the smile on her face.

"It is not quite as I would want it, but it will have to do." Lady Halifax sniffed and waved one hand in Clara's direction. "My daughter requires her gown now. And be quick about it, we are a little short on time."

"If you had not insisted that Clara do my hair on two further occasions, then we would not be in danger of being tardy," Joy remarked, rising from her chair, and walking across the room, quite missing the flash in her mother's eyes. "It was quite suitable the first time."

"*I* shall be the judge of that," came the sharp retort, as Lady Halifax stalked to the door. "Now do hurry up. The carriage is waiting, and I do not want us to bring the attention of the entire *ton* down upon us by walking in much later than any other!"

Joy sighed and nodded, turning back to where Clara was ready with her gown. Coming to London and seeking out a suitable match was not something she could get the least bit excited about, and this ball, rather than being a momentous one, filled with hope and expectation, felt like a heaviness on her shoulders. The sooner it was over, Joy considered, the happier she would be.

CHAPTER ONE

"*A*nd Lord Granger is seated there."

"Mm-hm."

Nudging Joy lightly, her mother scowled.

"You are not paying the least bit of attention! Instead, you are much too inclined towards staring! Though quite what you are staring at, I cannot imagine!"

Joy tilted her head but did not take her eyes away from what she had been looking at.

"I was wondering whether that lady there – the one with the rather ornate hairstyle – found it difficult to wear such a thing without difficulty or pain." The lady in question had what appeared to be a bird's nest of some description, adorned with feathers and lace, planted on one side of her head, with her hair going through it as though it were a part of the creation. There was also a bird sitting on the edge of the nest, though to Joy's eyes, it looked rather monstrous and not at all as it ought. "Surely it must be stuck to her head in some way." She could not keep a giggle back when the lady curtsied and then rose, only for her magnificent headpiece to wobble terribly. "Oh dear, perhaps it is not as well secured as it ought to be!"

"Will you stop speaking so loudly?"

The hiss from Lady Halifax had Joy's attention snapping back to her mother, a slight flush touching the edge of her cheeks as she realized that one or two of the other ladies near them were glancing in her direction. She had spoken a little too loudly for both her own good and her mother's liking.

"My apologies, Mama."

"I should think so!" Lady Halifax grabbed Joy's arm in a somewhat tight grip and then began to walk in the opposite direction of that taken by the lady with the magnificent hair. "Pray do not embarrass both me and yourself, with your hasty tongue!"

"I do not mean to," Joy muttered, allowing her mother to take her in whatever direction she wished. "I simply speak as I think."

"A trait I ought to have worked out of you by now, but instead, it seems determined to cling to you!" With a sigh, Lady Halifax shook her head. "Now look, do you see there?"

Coming to a hasty stop, Joy looked across the room, following the direction of her mother's gaze. "What is it that you wish me to look at, Mama?"

"Those young ladies there," came the reply. "Do you see them? They stand clustered together, hidden in the shadows of the ballroom. Even their own mothers or sponsors have given up on them!"

A frown tugged at Joy's forehead.

"I do not know what you are speaking of Mama."

"The wallflowers!" Lady Halifax turned sharply to Joy, her eyes flashing. "Do you not see them? They stand there, doing nothing other than adorning the wall. They are passed over constantly, ignored by the gentlemen of the *ton,* who care very little for their company."

"Then that is the fault of the gentlemen of the *ton,*" Joy answered, a little upset by her mother's remarks. "I do not think it is right to blame the young ladies for such a thing."

Lady Halifax groaned aloud, closing her eyes.

"Why do you willfully misunderstand? They are not wallflowers by choice, but because they are deemed as unsuitable for marriage, for one reason or another."

"Which, again, might not be their own doing."

"Perhaps, but all the same," Lady Halifax continued, sounding more exasperated than ever, "I have shown you these young ladies as a warning."

Joy's eyebrows shot towards her hairline.

"A warning?"

"Yes, that you will yourself become one such young lady if you do not begin to behave yourself and act as you ought." Moving so that she faced Joy directly, Lady Halifax narrowed her eyes a little. "You will find yourself standing there with them, doing nothing other than watching the gentlemen of London take various *other* young ladies out to dance, rather than showing any genuine interest in you. Would that not be painful? Would that not trouble you?"

The answer her mother wished her to give was evident to Joy, but she could not bring herself to say it. It was not that she wanted to cause her mother any pain, but that she could not permit herself to be false, not even if it would bring her a little comfort.

"It might," she admitted, eventually, as Lady Halifax let out another stifled groan, clearly exasperated. "But as I have said before, Mama, I do not wish to be courted by a gentleman who is unaware of my true nature. I do not see why I should hide myself away, simply so that I can please a suitor. If such a thing were to happen, if I were to be willing to act in that way, it would not make for a happy arrangement. Sooner or later, my real self would return to the fore, and then what would my husband do? It is not as though he could step back from our marriage. Therefore, I would be condemning both him and myself, to a life of misery. I do not think that would be at all agreeable."

"That is where you are wrong." Lady Halifax lifted her chin, though she looked straight ahead. "To be wed is the most satisfactory situation one can find oneself in, regardless of the circumstances. It is not as though you will spend a great deal of time with your husband so, therefore, you will never need to reveal your 'true nature', as you put it."

The more her mother talked, the more Joy found herself growing almost despondent, such was the picture Lady Halifax was painting of what would be waiting for her. She understood that yes, she was here to find a suitable match, but to then remove to her husband's estate, where she would spend most of her days alone and only be in her husband's company whenever he desired it, did not seem to Joy to be a very pleasant circumstance. That would be very dull indeed, would it not? Her existence would become small, insignificant, and utterly banal, and that was certainly *not* the future Joy wanted for herself.

"Now, do lift your head up, stand tall, and smile," came the command. "We must go and speak to Lord Falconer and Lord Dartford at once."

Joy hid her sigh by lowering her head, her eyes squeezing closed for a few moments. There was no time to protest, however, no time to explain to her mother that what had just been discussed had settled Joy's mind against such things as this, for Lady Halifax once more marched Joy across the room and, before she knew it, introduced Joy to the two gentlemen whom she had pointed out, as well as to one Lady Dartford, who was Lord Dartford's mother.

"Good evening." Joy rose from her curtsey and tried to smile, though her smile was a little lackluster. "How very glad I am to make your acquaintance."

"Said quite perfectly." Lord Dartford chuckled, his dark eyes sweeping across her features, then dropping down to her frame as Joy blushed furiously. "So, you are next in line to try your hand at the marriage mart?"

"Next in line?"

"Yes." Lord Dartford waved a hand as though to dismiss her words and her irritation, which Joy had attempted to make more than evident by the sweep of her eyebrow. "You have three elder sisters do you not?"

"Yes, I do." Joy kept her eyebrows lifted. "All of whom are all now wed and settled."

"And now you must do the same." Lord Dartford chuckled, but Joy did not smile. The sound was not a pleasant one. "Unfortunately, none of your sisters were able to catch my eye and, alas, I do not think that you will be able to do so either."

"Dartford!"

His mother's gasp of horror was clear, but Joy merely smiled, her stomach twisting at the sheer arrogance which the gentleman had displayed.

"That is a little forward of you, Lord Dartford," she remarked, speaking quite clearly, and ignoring the way that her mother set one hand to the small of her back in clear warning. "What is to say that I would have any interest in *your* company?"

This response wiped the smile from Lord Dartford's face. His dark eyes narrowed, and his jaw set but, much to Joy's delight, his friend began to guffaw, slapping Lord Dartford on the shoulder.

"You have certainly been set in your place!" Lord Falconer laughed as Joy looked back into Lord Dartford's angry expression without flinching. "And the lady is quite right, that was one of the most superior things I have heard you say this evening!"

"Only this evening?" Enjoying herself far too much, Joy tilted her head and let a smile dance across her features. "Again, Lord Dartford, I ask you what difference it would make to me to have a gentleman such as yourself interested in furthering their acquaintance with me? It is not as though I must simply accept every gentleman who comes to seek me out, is it? And I can assure you, I certainly would not accept you!"

Lord Falconer laughed again but Lord Dartford's

eyes narrowed all the more, his jaw tight and his frame stiff with clear anger and frustration.

"I do not think a young lady such as yourself should display such audacity, Miss Bosworth."

"And if I want your opinion, Lord Dartford, then I will ask you for it," Joy shot back, just as quickly. "Thus far, I do not recall doing so."

"We must excuse ourselves."

The hand that had been on Joy's back now turned into a pressing force that propelled her away from Lord Dartford, Lord Falconer, and Lady Dartford – the latter of whom was standing, staring at Joy with wide eyes, her face a little pale.

"Do excuse us."

Lady Halifax inclined her head and then took Joy's hand, grasping it tightly rather than with any gentleness whatsoever, dragging her away from the gentlemen she had only just introduced Joy to.

"Mama, you are hurting me!" Pulling her hand away, Joy scowled when her mother rounded on her. "Please, you must stop–"

"Do you know what you have done?"

The hissed words from her mother had Joy stopping short, a little surprised at her mother's vehemence.

"I have done nothing other than speak my mind and set Lord Dartford – someone who purports to be a gentleman – back into his place. I do not know what makes him think that I would have *any* interest in–"

"News of this will spread through London!" Lady Halifax blinked furiously, and it was only then that Joy saw the tears in her mother's eyes. "This is your very first

228 | ROSE PEARSON

ball on the eve of your come out, and you decide to speak with such force and impudence to the Earl of Dartford?"

A writhing began to roll itself around Joy's stomach.

"I do not know what you mean. I did nothing wrong."

"It is not about wrong or right," came the reply, as Lady Halifax whispered with force towards Joy. "It is about wisdom. You did not speak with any wisdom this evening, and now news of what you did will spread throughout society. Lady Dartford will see to that."

Joy lifted her shoulders and then let them fall.

"I could not permit Lord Dartford to speak to me in such a way. I am worthy of respect, am I not?"

"You could have ignored him!" Lady Halifax threw up her hands, no longer managing to maintain her composure, garnering the attention of one or two others nearby. "You did not have to say a single thing! A simple look – or a slight curl of the lip – would have sufficed. Instead, you did precisely what I told you not to do and now news of your audacity will spread through London. Lady Dartford is one of the most prolific gossips in all of London and given that you insulted her son, I fear for what she will say."

Joy kept her chin lifted.

"Mama, Lady Dartford was shocked at her own son's remarks to me."

"But that does not mean that she will speak of *him* in the same way that she will speak of you," Lady Halifax told her, a single tear falling as red spots appeared on her cheeks. "Do you not understand, Joy?"

"Lord Falconer laughed at what I said."

Lady Halifax closed her eyes.

"That means nothing, other than the fact that he found your remarks and your behavior to be mirthful. It will not save your reputation."

"I did nothing to ruin my reputation."

"Oh, but you did." A flash came into her mother's eyes. "You may not see it as yet, but I can assure you, you have done yourself a great deal of damage. I warned you, I *asked* you to be cautious and instead, you did the opposite. Now, within the first ball of the Season, your sharp tongue and your determination to speak as you please has brought you into greater difficulty than you can imagine." Her eyes closed, a heavy sigh breaking from her. "Mayhap you will become a wallflower after all."

Hmm, my mother always said my mouth would get me into trouble...and now Miss Bosworth could be in trouble! Check out the rest of the story on the Kindle store The Wallflower's Unseen Charm

Printed in Great Britain
by Amazon